Three Girls and a Baby

Rachel Schurig

Copyright © 2011 Rachel Schurig

ISBN: 1463541848
ISBN-13: 978-1463541842

For Madeline.

Thank you for ridiculous amounts of inspiration and support.

ACKNOWLEDGMENTS

Special thanks to Andrea, Michelle, Madeline, and Katy for all of your help, advice, and support.
Thank you to Nicholas J. Ambrose for proofreading services.
Book cover design by Scarlett Rugers Design 2011

www.scarlettrugers.com

Special thanks to my family for being so very supportive. I love you guys!

Like Ginny, I also worked as a nanny after college. However, I was lucky enough to work with many wonderful families. I thank them for letting me be a part of their children's lives.

Chapter One

Eight Weeks: Congratulations! By the eight week mark, most moms-to-be have discovered that they are in fact pregnant! Even if you have taken a test at home, it is important to make an appointment to visit your doctor at this point to confirm the pregnancy and check your overall health. At eight weeks of pregnancy, morning sickness (or all day sickness!) is very common. You may also feel more tired than usual throughout the day. You may even begin to notice a change in your waistline! Enjoy those skinny jeans while you still can, ladies! —Dr. Rebecca Carr, A Gal's Guide to a Fabulous First Pregnancy!

My life ended on a Saturday morning.

Oh okay, my life didn't end. Technically. But it sure felt like it did.

And yeah, I suppose you could make the argument that the whole mess technically began six weeks prior to that, when my ex-boyfriend, Josh, waltzed back into my life and created—with my willing and eager help—such havoc. But if you want to look at things that way, then I guess we could just as easily go back five years to when Josh and I started dating in the first place. To me though, that Saturday in January, the day I found

1

out, was really the beginning of the event that completely changed my life.

On that day, I woke to amazing smells wafting from the kitchen. Bacon, definitely bacon, and possibly...maple syrup? Yes, that was it. Snuggling deep into my duvet I smiled. Jen, my housemate, was cooking breakfast.

Annie, second housemate, and I were what you might call minimalists in the kitchen: pasta with sauce from a jar was an impressive meal for us. Jen, on the other hand, was a wonderful cook, though she had little opportunity to show off her skills. Jen was somewhat of a party girl and most of her dinners and lunches took place at smart restaurants with work colleagues—or with her latest conquests. But every so often she would wake up on a weekend morning determined and enthusiastic to set to work in the kitchen.

When Jen cooked, she never half-assed it. I could expect a breakfast feast of French toast, bacon, fruit salad...she probably would have even squeezed us fresh juice. Annie and I *love* these mornings.

After pulling on my robe I stumbled down the stairs, meeting Annie on the way. Her reddish blond hair was a frizzy uncombed mess around her shoulders, and she too was pulling on a robe.

"Morning," I yawned.

Annie nudged me with her elbow. "I'm sorry to have to tell you," she said in mournful tones, "but Jen is my favorite roommate. I would kick you out and never speak to you again if she wanted me to."

I nodded seriously. She had a point.

Arriving in the kitchen it was just as I expected: Jen was busy turning several pieces of French toast on the griddle. A large platter held cut oranges, strawberries, and melon chunks. The smell of bacon hung heavily in the air. Annie moaned and closed her eyes. "Jen Campbell, if you would have me I would turn lez for you, marry you, and do anything I could to keep you happy and cooking food for me."

Jen snorted. "Right, I'm sure. Grab some plates would you? These are about ready."

Per usual, Jen looked drop dead gorgeous, even for nine a.m. on a Saturday morning. While Annie and I were prone to lazing about all day in flannel PJs and fraying terry cloth robes, Jen was already wide awake in a turquoise silk dressing gown, her sleek brown hair neatly twisted up in a clip. It was pointless to even be jealous of her innate style and togetherness—I could just never pull it off.

As Annie got the plates from the cupboard, Jen pointed her spatula at me. "Silverware, lazy. Chop chop!"

Jen hummed to herself as she dipped another piece of bread. As I squeezed past her to reach the silverware drawer, I happened to glance down at the bowl holding the dipping mixture of eggs and milk. Immediately, I felt my stomach lurch violently and I knew I had seconds to get to the bathroom. Pushing away from the counter I stumbled as quickly as I could out of the kitchen and into the bathroom, falling to my knees in front of the toilet just in time.

When I was sure there was nothing left in my stomach to throw up, I flushed the toilet and leaned back against the cool tile wall. I felt shaky and sweaty. What was going on? I reached up to grab a Kleenex only to find the box empty. I knew there should be a new one under the sink: I had put it there myself only last week. I leaned over and opened the cabinet—but it wasn't a Kleenex box my fingers brushed first. It was a carton of tampons.

"Oh my God," I whispered. "Oh no, oh no..." Frantically I tried to count in my head. True, I had been a bit of a basket case lately, but I was fairly confident—no I was pretty damn sure—that I hadn't had a period in more than two months. And between then and now there was that night, that one single, horrible night with Josh...

For a moment I was sure that I was going to faint. The outlines of my fingers seemed to blur before my eyes and I felt my entire body start to tremble. *This can't be happening. Please God, let this not be happening.*

"Gin, you okay?" Annie called from the other side of the door. Okay? What did that word even mean? Would anything ever be okay again? "Ginny?" I could hear the worry growing in Annie's voice. How could I tell her what was happening? How could I tell her what I had done?

"Ginny, open the door, you're freaking me out." Her voice was firmer now, and somehow I found some strength in it.

Wiping my mouth I began to tell her that I was fine, but discovered I couldn't manage those words. "Come here please, Ann," I said instead. My voice sounded strange to my ears, the way it sounded when I heard myself on the answering machine.

I heard the knob turn as Annie peeked around the door. I didn't look up as she entered but I could picture the look of worry and confusion on her face as she took in my position on the floor. "What's wrong? Are you okay?" She was crouching in front of me before I could respond.

I looked up into her eyes, my very best friend, and I wished desperately that I wouldn't have to tell her what I suspected. I knew that Annie loved me, knew that there was no one better to have in my corner in a crisis. But there was something else I knew: Annie would judge me. She would be unable to understand how I could have been with Josh after everything. She would never say a word against me, but she would think it. She would think less of me, and I was terrified to see that in her eyes.

So, like the coward that I am, I closed mine.

"I think I'm pregnant," I whispered.

Chapter Two

Looking back on that Saturday, I would always be surprised that it was Jen that took control of the situation. Annie, usually so in charge of herself and the people around her, seemed almost as panicked as I was. After I told her she didn't talk for a very long time. When I finally opened my eyes and looked at her she appeared to be hyperventilating. It wasn't until Jen came to investigate that either of us managed to get up off the floor.

Now Annie was pacing endlessly around our tiny living room, literally ringing her hands. "You look like an old woman," I snapped from my seat on the couch, where Jen had deposited me with a glass of ginger ale while she went to put on clothes and find her car keys. Annie barely seemed to notice me, dazed as she was.

Jen walked briskly back into the room. "I'll be back in ten," she said, touching me briefly on the arm before she walked out of the front door. I heard her car start a moment later and leaned back into the couch, closing my eyes and trying not to lose it. After a few minutes, Annie finally seemed to remember that I was there.

"How do you feel now?" she asked, sitting down across from me on our old thrift store recliner.

"Scared shitless," I muttered.

"I'm sorry I freaked out," she said quietly. "I was just...shocked."

"You're not the only one."

"Do you...do you wanna tell me what happened?" she asked hesitantly.

"You mean whose is it?" I snapped.

She shrugged. "If you want to tell me."

I sighed deeply. "Josh came back, like, a month and a half ago. We talked, it got emotional, we kissed. Things got out of hand."

"Why didn't you tell me?" She sounded hurt.

"I was afraid you'd think I was pathetic," I admitted. "Hell, *I* thought I was pathetic. Even before it happened I knew it wouldn't mean anything had changed. I was kissing him, leading him to my room, and I knew it wouldn't change a thing. But I did it anyway."

"Is that...is that why he hasn't called lately?"

I looked at her sharply. "How do you know that?"

"It was pretty obvious you were still talking to him, Gin; we all knew it. And it was pretty obvious that it stopped." She paused, thinking. "Right around the time we had our little fight in fact."

"Yeah, he was here the week before that." I flinched. Even now the memory of that night could still cut deep. "After it was over I told him to leave me alone, to stop calling. When you got mad at me, I guess it only confirmed to me that I needed to try to move on."

"If I would have known that had just happened, I never would have said—"

"I know, don't worry about it. You snapped me out of it, it was a good thing."

She started to say something else, but we both heard a car pulling up into the drive. Jen was back.

She walked in, all business-like, and ushered me to the bathroom. "Okay, we're going to do this real fast and try not to think too much about it until it's done, deal?"

Honestly, I was a little too afraid of her and her new no-nonsense briskness to argue, so instead I meekly took the plastic stick she handed me out of the small box in her hand. "It says you pee here," she said, pointing, as she read aloud from the instructions. "Then you set the stick on the sink and wait for three minutes. No biggie." She squeezed my hand. "Come out when you're finished so we can wait together." I nodded mutely and she left.

They didn't give me the chance to come out. No sooner had I started pulling up my PJ pants and they were barging through the door. "Sorry, we were listening," Annie explained unabashedly. They pulled me down on the floor between the two of them, our backs leaning against the bathtub. Jen had set the timer on her iPhone and for a moment I couldn't take my eyes off the descending black numbers.

"This ceiling is really filthy," Jen noted mildly, her head tilted back.

"We're crap at cleaning," Annie agreed. "I told you we should have hired a cleaning service."

"Why would we spend good money to have someone else do something we're perfectly capable of doing ourselves?" Jen asked. This was a fight we had had before. Though, granted, never under quite these same circumstances.

"Do you think we could talk about something else?" I wondered aloud.

The girls were silent for a while. "That whole breakfast is probably ruined now," Jen said eventually. Annie laughed. Before I could decide if I was amused or annoyed, Jen's iPhone started beeping. "That's three minutes," she said quietly.

I couldn't move so instead I just sat there. "Um, do you want me to..?" Jen began. I nodded, closing my eyes. Annie squeezed my hand, hard, as Jen stood and reached for the test. I knew, before she even looked at it, what the verdict would be.

"Plus sign," she said evenly, calmly. "Pregnant."

* * *

I spent the rest of the day on the couch, buried underneath the thick quilt Jen's grandma had made for her about a million years ago. Annie and Jen kept trying to get me to eat or talk to them. I kept telling them to fuck off. I watched about five episodes of *Top Chef* (there was a marathon on) before Jen finally took control, again, this time by wrestling the remote away from me and turning off the television. Annie joined in and stole the quilt and my pillow. Then they each took an arm and pulled me into a sitting position, taking a seat on my either side so I couldn't flee.

"I know that you don't want to talk about this," Jen started. "But I think we should."

"Why?" I asked petulantly. "Why can't we just forget about it?"

"Ginny," Annie said patiently, in her talking-to-toddlers voice. "Forgetting about it won't make it go away."

"You don't have to decide anything yet," Jen continued. "But you should probably start thinking about your options, and about getting in touch with Josh."

"I'm not telling Josh," I said quickly. "No way."

"What are you talking about?" Jen asked. "You have to tell him."

"No, no way. He'll think I did it on purpose. Everyone will. They know I was desperate to get him back; they'll think this was my plan all along."

"Don't be ridiculous," Jen scoffed, at the same time Annie said, "Well, was it?"

Jen glared at her. "Kidding, kidding!" Annie said quickly, holding up her hands.

"Ginny, regardless of what he, or anyone else, thinks of your motives, you have a huge decision to make, and he should have some input."

"What do you mean, huge decision?" I asked Jen. She and Annie exchanged a look.

"I mean, what are you going to do about the baby?"

"Do?" Everything felt fuzzy to me and I couldn't understand what she was talking about.

"Ginny, you need to decide if you want to have this baby," Jen said softly. "And if you are, how you're going to take care of it."

I stared at her, her words finally sinking in. She wanted me to decide if I was going to have it or...or get rid of it. Get rid of Josh's baby. I shook my head quickly. "I'm having it. You know I could never have an...an..."

"An abortion?" Annie said bluntly.

"Yeah. I couldn't do that. It would be...it's wrong."

"Aw, how sweet. Catherine would be so proud," Annie said mildly. Catherine was my mother.

"I don't think proud will quite be what she feels when she hears about this," I moaned. "Oh God, I'm going to have to tell my *mother*!"

"And your dad!" Annie said cheerfully. I glared at her, as did Jen.

"You're really not helping," she hissed.

"I'm trying to lighten the mood!" Annie protested.

"Listen, you guys," I said. "I get that I have a lot to think about, and a lot to decide. But it's kind of a lot to take in all at once. And I don't have to figure anything out tonight, do I?"

"No, of course not," Jen agreed. "I just want to make sure that you know...Annie and I...well." Jen seemed uncomfortable. I looked at Annie, confused.

"Oh Christ, Jen, you're allowed to get a little sappy when you've just found out your best friend is knocked up," Annie scoffed. Then she turned to me, her eyes solidly on mine. "What she's tying to say, Gin, is that whatever you decide, we're here. Right here. We'll help you with whatever you need. You don't have to worry, okay?"

Jen grabbed my hand, squeezing it and nodding. I felt a lump come to my throat. I loved these girls so much. "Okay," I whispered. We sat in silence for a moment, each too overwhelmed to say more.

Jen pulled herself together first. "Ginny," she asked kindly, "would you like me to turn *Top Chef* back on?"

I smiled for the first time since that morning. "Yes, please."

Chapter Three

Six short months ago, my life had been very different. Before graduation, before moving home, before losing Josh. Back then, a pregnancy surprise probably would have been a cause for celebration: two people creating life from their love for each other, and all that crap. But now...Now I was alone.

Alright, alright, I'm being melodramatic again. I'm not alone: I have Annie and Jen, the two best girlfriends anyone could hope for.

Annie Duncan and I grew up together. I know we became friends in kindergarten but I honestly can't even remember the first time we met—it seems like we've always been friends. It should surprise no one that Annie is an actress: she's loud, funny, expressive. Annie can come across as cynical and sarcastic, and I know that a lot of people are intimidated by her—but if you're lucky enough to get to know her, you'll find that she's the perfect girlfriend. There's no one I know more loyal than Annie.

We met Jen Campbell in high school, when her family moved to Royal Oak, the small suburban town outside of Detroit where Annie and I grew up. Jen fit in with the two of us perfectly. We share the same sense of humor, the same interest in fashion. Most

importantly, the three of us share a love of *fun*—
parties, traveling, concerts, adventure. It wasn't long
before we were inseparable.

Annie, Jen and I had moved in together the
previous July, shortly after graduating from college.
Our little yellow rental house was perfect for us—
enough room for us each to have privacy but not so big
that three domestically challenged party girls would
have to do much housework. The house is in Ferndale,
a short drive from Detroit and our home town. Best of
all, we're in walking distance of several bars and nice
restaurants, which was a major selling point for us.

We had talked about living together post-
graduation for ages. The three of us had remained
close throughout college, though we'd all been at
different schools. Having gone away to State with
Josh, I never had the opportunity to live with friends,
or any girls for that matter. When it finally happened,
I was almost giddy—a cute house, my two best friends.
I imagined it would be like a constant sleepover. We'd
eat ice cream, watch movies, and I'd be over Josh in
weeks.

And at first that was exactly how it went. There
were long tearful chats about my break-up. There were
rom-com movie marathons. There was much drinking
of wine and late night fast food runs. There were even
impromptu dance parties in the living room (brought
on by the drinking of said wine). If my life were a chick
flick, this period would have passed as a musical
montage about the strength of female friendships, and
its ability to heal the wounds left by bastard men.

But as time went on I realized something: I wasn't over Josh. Not at all. I missed him, almost in a detached sort of way. It started to feel like I was on a vacation and had left my boyfriend at home. The break-up didn't seem real. I was not over him.

Soon this fact became clear to Annie and Jen as well. I could tell they were losing patience with me, that the tearful chats were becoming more and more one-sided. Their advice slowly shifted from compassionate and bracing to frustrated and short. From their point of view it was simple: my relationship had ended, it had been months, it was time to Move On.

What they didn't understand, what no one seemed to understand, is that it's impossible to move on when you don't really want to. And it's impossible to want to move on when you're still in love.

* * *

Josh had appeared at our house, completely unannounced, back in November.

It wasn't that we hadn't talked since the break-up. Every few weeks or so he would text, or, just as often, he would call. Sometimes it was when he was drunk. Usually it was late. But always it ended the same way — I would answer, thrilled, sure he was going to change his mind, sure this was the first step to him coming back. We would either flirt or argue. And okay, if I'm being totally honest, a few times when we were both drinking we ended up having phone sex. But always, always, we would hang up, still broken, still over, and I would lay on my bed, alone and too empty to even cry.

I was powerless to stop it. When he texted, when he called, all I had to do was hit delete, not answer. I could tell him that I needed time, that it was painful for me to hear from him—Josh would have understood. Hell, I could even tell Annie or Jen, who would get me drunk and physically keep me from my phone. But I never had the strength. If he called, I would answer. If he wanted to throw me crumbs, even soul-crushing ones, I would take them, grateful.

I was powerless to stop it.

So you can imagine what happened to my sliver of willpower when he actually showed up at my house.

I left work that night in November, exhausted as usual, and anxious only to get home and into my pajamas. I had received texts from both Annie and Jen that afternoon, letting me know not to expect them until late, if at all. Jen had a date—big surprise—and Annie had been recruited to help hang lights for an upcoming show down at the Trinity Theater in the city. I had a feeling her willingness to help had as much to do with the gorgeous tech director as it did with her desire to earn some extra cash.

Often, I was the first one home, and in those days I cherished the few moments without the girls. I could put on PJ pants, lay on the couch and cry, and never once did I have to worry that I was making my friends nervous.

When they were home, particularly when Jen was home, I had to act engaged. I had to try to chat and to laugh. I had to try very hard not burst into tears at the smallest provocation.

But on that Friday, for once, I wasn't looking forward to the time alone. The thought of sitting on the couch all night, thinking of Josh, watching lame movies for the millionth time...it made me feel anxious in a way I didn't understand. I had a fleeting desire to get dressed up, go out to a bar with Annie and Jen— we'd done that a few times since moving in together. Ferndale was kind of a trendy town and as such it had a lot of new and interesting bars and clubs. I usually had fun once I got a few drinks in me, but it always took a lot of convincing for Annie and Jen to get me to agree to go out at all.

I smiled slightly to myself as I pulled onto our street. Maybe I was turning a corner if the thought of actually going out sounded better to me than staying in alone. Then I sighed. Corner turned or not, I was still going to be on my own for the foreseeable future.

Preoccupied with my thoughts, I didn't notice the car parked in front of the house until I had pulled into the driveway. As I turned to grab my purse from the passenger seat I caught sight of it in the rearview mirror. My breath caught in my throat.

The car, a dark blue Chevy with a small dent in the side door, was as familiar to me as my own, and the man stepping out from the driver's side door had haunted my thoughts every day for the last three months. It was Josh.

Chapter Four

I couldn't wrap my mind around what was happening. Josh was sitting at the kitchen table, as comfortable and unruffled as I had ever seen him. Josh, here. Josh, in my house.

I tried to steady my hands as I busied myself with the wine glasses. "Red or white?" I was proud that there was no tremor in my voice.

"Red, please," he replied. "Thanks."

I brought the wine to table and sat down across from him. I couldn't stop my fingers from fidgeting with the stem of my glass. God, he looked good. His hair was longer than I remembered, the extra inch making his blond curls more prominent. Josh was tall, 6'2", and his body looked slightly thicker folded up in a kitchen chair that was more accustomed to the females who lived here. He was wearing a dark olive sweater that seemed to darken his green eyes, and jeans. I suppressed a sigh. I had always loved him in dark jeans.

"Gin," he said softly, reaching across and grasping my wrist lightly, stopping my fingers from taping against the glass. "Relax. I'm not going to hurt you."

I swallowed and looked up into his eyes. There was that familiar twinkle there, that flash of amusement, and I felt myself relax. I knew this man, better than anyone, and suddenly it didn't seem strange or overwhelming that he was there. It seemed normal—it seemed like us. I smiled.

"That's better." He released my wrist. "So. Ginny. How've you been?"

"Oh, you know. Same old." I promised myself I wouldn't tell him hard it'd been, how much I missed him every single day.

"How's the job? Still driving you crazy?" He seemed genuinely interested, like he used to be when we talked, back in the days before the mere sight of me made him exhausted (his words).

"Oh yeah, crazier than ever. Maybe even insane." Josh laughed softly and I felt my heart clench. *Keep it light.* I urged myself. "How about you? What's new? You in town to visit your folks?" *Stop asking questions, you're babbling!*

"No, actually. I came down to see you."

I felt the world freeze. "Why?" I whispered.

He was quiet for a moment. "I miss you, Gin." He wasn't quite whispering, but his voice was soft. I stared at him, but this time *he* wasn't meeting *my* eyes.

"What does that mean, Josh?"

"I don't know." He picked up his glass and gulped the wine. "I don't fucking know. Everything that happened, everything I said...I meant it, Gin. We stopped being good for each other."

Why was he doing this to me? Telling me he missed me but he didn't want me? Suddenly I felt angry. For the first time since this happened I stopped feeling sorry for myself. I didn't feel heartbroken—I felt *pissed.*

"What. The. Fuck. Josh?" My voice was hoarse, tight. "You break up with me, you tell me we can't be together. You *know* I didn't feel that way, you know I still love you!" I was shouting now. "But you keep calling me, always keeping me strung along. And then you show up here, in my house, to tell me that you miss me but nothing's changed? And you don't know what it means? What the fuck?"

He stood suddenly, pushing his chair back so roughly it scraped against the tile. "Do you think this has been easy for me, Ginny?" he yelled back. "I've been in love with you since I was seventeen years old. Yes, things changed, they got fucked up!" He leaned down close to me, his face hard, twisted, and so not like Josh. "And you *know* that wasn't all my fault. You know the problems went both ways."

I closed my eyes. He was right, completely right. Everything he was saying was the stuff I had tried for so long to bury deep inside. I had let people, especially Annie and Jen, believe I was the victim. But I knew, as he did, the role I had played in our break-up.

"Do you think that I wouldn't give anything to be able to just forgive you? Just forget about everything that happened?" He stopped suddenly and sighed, clearly trying to regain control. "It wasn't right to stay with you anymore," he said softly. "But that doesn't mean that those feelings all went away. So I miss you, okay?"

"Okay," I whispered, as the tears welled up under my closed eyelids and began to slip down my cheeks.

"Ginny, please, don't," he said, his own voice starting to shake. "Don't cry!" He knelt in front of my chair, forcing me to look at him. "Please."

"I miss you too," I sobbed. "That's what I should have said first, Josh. I miss you so much!"

He grabbed me and held me close, burying his face in my hair. I held him tight, squeezing until I could hardly breathe.

"I'm sorry, Ginny," he said fervently. "I'm so, so sorry." His lips were brushing against my hair now, against my head, and I melted into it, willing him to continue. His lips brushed my cheek and then, suddenly, we were kissing.

His lips were hot against mine, pressing hard. It was heaven and so much pain, all rolled into one. I couldn't have stopped if I wanted to, and I had never wanted anything less. I knew what this would cost me later, once he was gone again. But I couldn't help myself. I loved him, and he was here.

He stood, pulling me with him in one fluid move. Never breaking the kiss he pulled me into the hall, pressing me into the wall. His lips felt fierce against mine, as if he was battling something. I wondered if it were me.

Finally he pulled away, drawing in a ragged breath. "I shouldn't do this to you. I *know* I shouldn't do this to you."

"I don't care, Josh." My voice was low and tense. "I don't want you to leave. Not tonight." I looked up into his eyes and the heat I saw there made my stomach flip. It had been so long. "Please." I pulled his face back down to mine, kissing him with every bit of desperation I had within me. Then I took his hand and led him to my bedroom.

* * *

I lay awake for a long time afterward. I wasn't sure what I was feeling. Part of me was still angry—at him, at myself—and part of me was terribly, terribly sad, knowing he would see this as a mistake, knowing he would still leave. But a large part of me, a growing part, felt calm. I was beginning to understand some things about the situation that hadn't ever dawned on me.

"You awake?" Josh whispered in the darkness.

"Yeah," I replied. "How you feeling?"

"Sad," he said softly. "I wish...I wish we could just go back to where we used to be." His words were followed by a long silence as we both processed that.

"But we can't," I finally said. "Right? That's the whole point of all of this, isn't it? We can't have a relationship based on what we used to be."

He didn't answer. I didn't really need him to.

"Josh, I love you, and I want to give us another shot. But I don't think you want that...and I don't think either of us has really changed enough to make it worth trying. Have we?"

"No," he said, his voice now so soft I could barely hear him.

"Then I'm gonna need you to do something for me." I kept my back to him, knowing I would lose my nerve if I could see him. "I need you to leave now. And when you walk out that door..." The words were in danger of getting stuck in my throat. I took a deep breath and pushed on. "When you leave here, I need you to not call me for a while, okay? No texts, no dropping by, no emails. I need to not hear from you."

He was quiet for a long time. "That's going to be really hard," he finally replied.

"For me too. But I think we both know it's the only way things are going to change, for either of us. You need to figure out what you want and I need to figure out how to stop..." I trailed off.

"Stop what?"

"Stop being this person. This needy, obsessed, unhappy person." I took a deep breath, unsure of how much to say. "For so long, all I've wanted is you, us. I need to find out what there is to me, without you. Does that make sense?"

"Yeah," he said, and his voice was sad. "I want you to be happy, Ginny. You used to be so, so happy...you used to be...I don't know, luminous. When we first met, that's how I thought of you. All lit up and glowing, and so out of my reach."

I chuckled bitterly. "Funny how things turn out."

"That's still you," he said, leaning over and kissing my cheek. "I know it is."

I heard the bed creak as he got up, heard him gather his clothes. He paused at the door and I forced myself not to look at him, scared that I would throw myself back into his arms and beg him to stay. "Take care of yourself," he finally said. And then the door was clicking shut, and he was gone.

Chapter Five

"Alright, that's it, Ginny," Annie snapped, her voice as cold as I had ever heard it. I looked up, surprised. Annie never talked to me in that tone.

"What?" I asked, genuinely confused.

"Did you even hear a word that I said?" Annie was pissed. It kind of freaked me out a little.

"Um, I guess I was distracted..." I trailed off. It was about two weeks after Josh's visit, and I had been staring, completely unseeing, at the television screen when Annie got home, all excited about something.

Up until that point, my depression had been pretty severe, but after Josh left, it shifted quickly into downright debilitating. I would lay on my bed and stare into space for long stretches of time. At work (I'm a nanny) I would completely zone out while the kids played, having no idea how much time had passed when I finally came to.

I hadn't told anyone what had happened. I knew the girls would not approve of what I'd done and, to be honest, it hurt so much to even think about our goodbye I couldn't imagine being able to talk about it. But I sure as hell relived it a lot—over and over. And so, okay, I hadn't really been listening when Annie bustled in and started talking.

25

"Oh, big surprise. You were distracted," she snarled now. "What a nice change for you."

Yup, pissed.

"Annie, I'm sorry. I know I've been out of it, but there's something I should tell you—"

"No, Ginny, there's something I'm trying to tell *you*! I had a fucking audition. And it went really fucking awesome. And, as my best friend, that should mean something to you!"

I was stunned. "Ann, that's great! What's the show?"

"I just told you the show! Five minutes ago! But you weren't listening!" She was shouting now, and I was shocked to see tears brimming in her eyes. "Because you never, ever fucking listen to me anymore. You just sit there in your little bubble, enjoying your pathetic drama. I am so sick of it!"

I had no idea what to do. I knew she was right, but what could I say?

As it turned out, she saved me the trouble of answering. Slamming the front door hard enough to shake the windows, she was gone.

* * *

I sat completely still for a long time after Annie left. I felt shocked and unsteady. I knew I had been irritating the girls, I knew they were fed up with my constant sadness. But never had I realized that it went farther than that. I hadn't thought that in my misery I was actually hurting them. I was a shitty friend.

Suddenly I was sick of it all. Sick of sitting in this house, sick of this damn couch. Sick of *myself*. I needed to get out. I pulled on my winter coat, grabbed my iPod, and headed out into the cold.

I walked for more than an hour. The biting cold air felt amazing in my lungs. I found one of my old running playlists on my iPod and the loud, pulsing rock was the perfect soundtrack to the scenery of frozen lawns and trees around me.

I felt my senses waking up. It seemed like everything had been fuzzy for so long, the colors of my world muted and blurred. When had fall turned to winter? Fall was my favorite season, and it had passed without me noticing. I reached a small playground, deserted in the cold, and found a bench. I sat down heavily and allowed my mind to wander, back to the places where I had been trying so hard to keep away from.

So much had happened since the summer, so much had changed for me. I had changed. Josh had been right when he talked about the way I used to be, I knew that. There was a time, believe it or not, when I was the vivacious one. I was on homecoming court in high school, for God's sake. I used to be loud, funny, bold. I was a varsity track star, the fastest runner in my class. I stood out in a crowd, people noticed me. It was part of the reason why Annie, Jen and I had gotten along so well: we were the fun girls. We went to parties, we danced, we talked and laughed, loud and obvious, never caring who was looking at us or what they thought. The three of us were as tight as three girls could be, but we had tons of other friends too, other groups that we moved through seamlessly, easily.

When Josh and I first got together, back in high school, he was almost painfully shy. Few people who know him now understand quite how self-conscious he really was, just below the surface, and how much that used to affect him. I was the one who pulled him out of that; I was the one who changed him from shy, awkward wallflower to fun, popular guy. Just his being with me changed the way people thought of him. I know it's horribly conceited to think of myself this way, but it's also true. Or at least, it *was* true, a very long time ago.

Josh Stanley was known at our school for being a really talented writer, mostly working on short stories and a little poetry. What had first caught my attention about him was the way I would always see him around the school—in the back of our classes, out on the lawn, lounging in the hallway— his head bent over a notebook, his curly hair falling into his eyes as he wrote furiously. He seemed a million miles away from me, from all of the ridiculousness of high school. I wanted to bring him back, or, better still, force him to take me with him into his world.

I had dated a lot of boys before Josh. I was the only child of two very conservative parents. My mom and dad were a lot older than the parents of most of my friends. I think they had given up on kids years before I came along and I had come as something of a shock to them. They didn't seem to enjoy parenting too much, and they certainly didn't seem to enjoy me much at all. They were strict and demanding, religious and rigid in their beliefs on how I should act.

I rebelled. I rebelled hardcore, from the time I was a kid all the way through high school. I drank, I kissed boys, I got my nose pierced. I wound up my dad by telling him I was becoming a socialist. I pretended to be a lesbian for a week just to see if my mom's head would explode. I broke curfew and dressed all in black and flirted with anyone who would look at me. I left condoms out on my dresser in full view of anyone walking down the hall. I told my mom I thought marriage was like slavery for a woman—I planned to sleep with whoever I wanted and concentrate my efforts on a career.

Josh made me see that all of that was bullshit.

I had initially tried to get his attention the way I had with all the other boys. I flirted, I dressed provocatively, I showered him with attention. He was always kind to me, he paid me attention when I demanded it, but it never went further than politeness. All of that—my entire life really—changed the night of Amanda Dowger's house party.

It was the middle of junior year. I had been trying, without success, to win Josh over for the better part of two months. The less interested he seemed, the more determined I got. I remember Jen telling me if I didn't get in his pants or move on soon, she was going to disown me. I determined that night, the night of Amanda's party, would be the night I made it happen. I knew Josh was going to be there so I dressed to the nines: tight pants, cleavage, sleek hair, tons of make-up. When I got into her car Annie informed me that I looked like a prostitute. I kissed her on the cheek.

When we got to the party I put my plan into motion. It was simple, if moronic: I was going to get drunk and flirt with as many guys as I could to show Josh what he was missing. By ten thirty I was well on my way, at least in the drunk and moronic categories. Scanning the room, I found him sitting on the couch, talking casually to some sophomore in our creative writing class. Knowing he'd be watching me, I made my way to the center of the room, where people were dancing. I picked a random football player and started dancing, grinding and being, in a word, slutty.

After a few songs I decided to test the waters, see how Josh had been affected by my plan. I flopped down on the couch next to him, sitting as close as I could, and leaned my whole body into him. "I'm *so* drunk," I giggled in my most girlish voice.

"Ginny," he said quietly. "Why are you doing this?"

I looked up into his solemn face, surprised. "What...what do you mean?" I stammered. He leaned down, so our faces were close together.

"You're so much better than this. You should knock it off."

His words sent me reeling. It was like he had cut me down to my core, like he had seen through me in a way no one ever had. I felt off-balance; I was both elated and not at all sure that I liked this. Suddenly, I realized I was going to be sick. I pushed off from the couch and ran through the front door, retching into the bushes, reactionary tears streaming down my face.

When I finished I sank down to my knees on the cold grass. It was only then that I realized Josh was standing right next to me, maybe had been the whole time. He knelt down, too, and held out his cup, offering me a sip of his Coke.

"I was thinking I might get out of here," he said, as if nothing had happened. "I wondered if maybe you wanted to go with me, get some coffee or something." I stared at him, completely shocked for the second time that night.

Josh stood. "Come on," he said firmly, holding out his hand. "Let's go." And reaching down, he pulled me back up off the cold grass and into his world.

*　　*　　*

Sitting on the cold park bench in November, I felt wetness on my cheeks. I hadn't let myself think of that night in so long. It was the beginning for us, but it also explained how we would end, if you knew what to look for in the story. Five years later, we would be in almost the same place, with me desperate, doing everything I could think of to hang on to Josh. But just like before, the more I tried, the farther away he moved. And this time when I messed up, when I took it too far, he refused to be there to pull me back up.

Chapter Six

Ten Weeks: At ten weeks you will most likely be experiencing many of the more annoying aspects of pregnancy: morning sickness, acne, mood swings, and body aches. You'll probably also find that your bladder demands more frequent trips to the bathroom. Never fear, ladies, this part doesn't last forever! If you haven't already done so, it's important to see you doctor soon and have a complete physical done. Enjoy these precious months, mommies-to-be!
—Dr. Rebecca Carr, *A Gal's Guide to a Fabulous First Pregnancy!*

I have never felt so disgusting in my entire life. Seriously. I had a horrible bout of stomach flu once when I was sixteen, and I've had more killer hangovers than your average girl. But not even the worst hangover in the world could compare with this.

I was sick every single morning for the next two weeks. Not only that, but I was often sick in the afternoons, too. And the early evening. And sometimes, for good measure, I was sick at night. I don't know how I was managing to keep enough calories in my system to keep me conscious, I was throwing up so often.

And then there was my bladder. I had to pee, like, every thirty minutes, without fail. Even at night, I was waking up constantly to go to the bathroom. So annoying. And exhausting.

The weirdest smells bothered me. I couldn't stand to be around broccoli, eggs, or apples. I came home one night to Annie heating up potato soup, which I normally loved, and decided right then and there that potatoes were going to be a no-go for the duration of this pregnancy.

This pregnancy. God. I still couldn't get used to it. I was *pregnant.*

I still hadn't told Josh. I came close a few times, even going so far as to pick up my cell and pull up his number, but I never went through with it. I was, quite literally, terrified to tell him. I hadn't told my parents yet either. I had stopped caring about their opinion, for the most part, ages ago. They had been disappointed with me for so long, it had seemed stupid to continue to worry about it. But this was going to ratchet that disappointment up to an unprecedented level, and I found myself scared of their reaction for the first time in many, many years.

And then there were the money worries. How on earth was I going to pay for this baby? Since graduation Annie and I both been working as nannies for rich families in Bloomfield Hills, a very swanky neighborhood nearby. I had had no clue what I had wanted to do after college, and Annie had found that well-paid acting jobs were pretty scarce in the Detroit area. Nannying was meant to be a way to earn some money while we tried to figure out a better plan.

The pay wasn't horrible but it wasn't anything to raise a baby with. Plus, I had pretty crappy insurance, some young-adult bare minimum plan that Annie and I had signed up for after graduation had booted us from our parents' coverage—the rich families did not provide benefits. Jen, the only one of us with a real job, had fabulous insurance, and she volunteered to participate in fraud, letting me pretend to be her. I declined, but appreciated the offer—Jen didn't like to break rules.

Even if I could afford medical coverage, what about what came next? How could I pay for diapers, food, toys, clothes? I could barely afford to take care of myself. I didn't have completely excessive tastes, but I did enjoy my clothes, and my make-up, and most of all, my shoes. I had been known to take on extra hours at work for the sole purpose of affording a new pair of shoes. That habit would have to be cut out. How on earth was I going to live without new shoes?

These thoughts were so depressing that I tried to not think about any of it too much. Annie told me that this was denial, and I had better snap out of it soon. Jen kept trying to corner me with her laptop, insistent that we needed to start researching social programs for poor, single mothers so we could Make A Plan. I didn't want to think about plans, or welfare, or any of it. So I didn't.

I did go to the doctor, though, but only because Jen tricked me into thinking we were going to the movies. She said an early doctor visit was very important—apparently she was reading baby books on my behalf—and she wouldn't take no for an answer. She even found an Ob-Gyn that would take my insurance—with a hefty co-pay, but it was better than nothing.

The visit went fine; I could almost pretend it was simply a physical, like I used to have every year when I was on the track team. They did basic stuff like take my blood pressure and measure me. They also asked a million questions about my health and habits. The doctor was pleased I didn't smoke, but told me in no uncertain terms that my love affair with pinot grigio was on hold for the next seven-and-a-half-months.

He did some blood work as well, and an ultrasound. I couldn't see anything yet, or even hear the heart beat. There had been a part of me, a small, stupid, in-denial part, that was hoping it was all a misunderstanding. At home tests could be wrong, and maybe the sickness was the result of some mysterious, life-threatening illness—one could dream, right? But the doctor assured me that I was, in fact, pregnant, killing any remaining hope I might have had.

* * *

The last Friday in January started out like every other morning: I was late for work. I knew that it took me, on average, sixteen minutes to rush down Woodward Avenue from my house to the Conrad house, where I would spend the day babysitting. This meant that I should leave at least twenty minutes before my seven thirty start time to be safe. In practice though, I generally gave myself ten minutes, meaning, of course, that I was almost always late, a trend that was not helped at all by my near-constant morning sickness.

The Conrad house was its usual before-school chaos when I finally rushed through the door. Christopher and Madeline, ages ten and eight, were fighting over who got to finish the chocolate milk—Madeline dressed, but with messy hair, and Christopher still in his PJs. Jill, also in PJs, was covered in maple syrup and crying to get out of her high chair.

In the middle of this was Kelsie, their mother, sitting at the kitchen table with a grimace on her face and her head resting on one hand. "You're late," she muttered, looking up at me. Inwardly I marveled at the nerve of the woman who regularly came home forty-five minutes late with no explanation. Outwardly I smiled and said a cheerful good morning to the kids.

"Mommy, braid my hair! You promised!" demanded Madeline in a whiny, bossy voice that made me cringe. *Why would anyone let their kid talk like that?* I wondered for the hundredth time.

Kelsie abruptly pushed her chair back from the table. "Mommy's late for an appointment," she said briskly. "Ginny will help you." And before I could even say a word, she was gone.

I bit back a curse. The room was a mess, the kids weren't ready, and they needed to leave for school in fifteen minutes. When I was hired, Kelsie had told me she would take the kids to school on her way out each day, leaving me at home with Jill. Any changes to that plan were supposed to be communicated ahead of time. Yeah, right.

I had held some babysitting jobs throughout college to help pay my way, but this was my first experience taking care of a child full-time, and certainly my first experience working for people with such showy wealth. The Conrads lived in a huge house, and everything in it, from the furniture to the dishes to the black and white professional photographs on the mantle, bespoke wealth and good taste. Very little of the house felt like a place where children lived.

However, the Conrads did indeed have children— three of them. Christopher and Madeline were in school most of the day and thus didn't factor into my daily responsibilities much—or at least, they weren't supposed to. My primary job was taking care of three-year-old Jill.

Jill was a doll. She was exactly the child I had always dreamed of having myself. Her white-blond hair curled in spirals so perfect they almost didn't seem real. She was generally cheerful and giggly and had huge blue eyes that could melt me on my worst day. Because of the aforementioned showy wealth of her parents, she had a gorgeous pink and white bedroom filled with the best Pottery Barn furniture money could buy. On a regular basis I encouraged her to play dress up with her J Crew Baby wardrobe. Those were the times I liked my job.

Unfortunately, those times were rather scarce.

When Annie had first told me she could get me a job with the friend of the woman she was working for, I was pretty geeked. I envisioned myself in a big, beautiful house, chauffeuring kids from one activity to the other in a luxurious SUV, using nap times to catch up on my reality TV habit. I pictured hand-me-downs from designer closets and generous, expensive gifts for birthdays and Christmas.

What I did not imagine was spoiled kids screaming until they got their way; parents assuming I would work late with no notice; or being expected to pick up dry cleaning, return bottles, wrap gifts, cook meals. And what I certainly did not expect was that I would be working full-time for a woman with one child at home and no job.

At the time, I had just graduated and I had no idea what I wanted to do next. My degree, English Lit, didn't seem to be opening up many doors for me career-wise.

To be completely honest, I had always expected to be married by this point in my life: deciding on a career hadn't really factored into my post-graduation plans. Since I was moving home anyway, and Josh wasn't coming with me, the nannying job seemed like the best option available. So now, here I was, in a rich woman's house, racing to get her kids cleaned up and ready for school while she, more than likely, was headed for a mani-pedi.

I sighed and, in my meanest take-no-shit-from-spoiled-brats voice, ordered Christopher to go get dressed and brush his teeth. He did what he was told, as was usually the case when I got strict with him—since his parents never took any control over his behavior he always seemed surprised into obedience when I did so. Madeline could be trickier—though she was often whiny and demanding I detected a lot of hurt in her little brown eyes. On many occasions when I had worked late, or sat on weekends, and had tucked her into bed, she would beg me to stay with her in the dark, cuddling into me and squeezing tight. She was the middle child of parents who never seemed to have time for her.

"Okay, Maddie-loo-loo," I singsonged at her, making her giggle. "Let's make a deal. If you can get your teeth brushed and your shoes on before I count to fifty, I'll braid your hair. Otherwise it's a piggies day, okay?" She nodded enthusiastically at me, eager to avoid piggies, otherwise known as pigtails, which she hated. As she ran off, I turned to Jill, who was now beaming up at me through the syrup mess on her face.

"You, missy, are gross," I told her, grabbing a dish towel and getting it wet. As I attacked her face I tickled her tummy to keep her from squirming and fighting me. By the time Christopher came back down, dressed and ready, I had Jill mostly cleaned and had her coat bundled over her PJs. I decided the kitchen could wait, so I sent Chris to get his shoes on while I quickly braided Madeline's hair.

When I finally got everyone shepherded out of the house and strapped into their car seats I was pleased to see we were only running a few minutes late. Madeline was happy with her hair, I had reminded

Chris to bring his homework, and Jill was leaving only trace amounts of syrup on everything she touched.

My job may have been frustrating, demeaning, and downright annoying, but you couldn't deny that I was damn good at it.

* * *

Once the older kids were gone, the rest of the day calmed down somewhat, though I was hit by another bout of morning sickness once I'd gotten Jill home. To be honest, work was this hard on a daily basis now. I was more tired than ever, because I was sleeping so badly. Being sick every morning did not help my chronic lateness. Most days, I was sick again once I got there—I was grateful, for once, that Kelsie was gone so often. I had no idea how she was going to take my news.

At home in the evenings, I did everything I could to keep my mind off the pregnancy and all the stressful worry that went with it. Annie convinced me to keep up with our yoga, and it ended up being the only time my body felt normal. It helped with the aches and the nausea and I wished I could afford to go more often. I had to stop running because it made me have to pee even more often, but Jen insisted I take a walk with her every evening. She also tried to make me eat balanced and healthy meals. She was staying home just about every night now, and she cooked for me all the time. Normally, this would have made me tremendously happy, but now most food made me hurl, so I couldn't quite enjoy her efforts.

Our Netflix queue was getting quite a work out these days as I felt movies were a great escape. Jen did not approve of my constant escaping—she was still bugging me to Make A Plan—but I was so pathetic and sick all the time I was able to convince her I deserved it.

When I finally got home that Friday, Annie and I both curled up on the couch to watch *Sex and the City*. It was, by far, Our-Favorite-Show-Of-All-Time, and I found it was very easy to tune out those worried voices in my head when I was watching it. Jen had bought me the entire series on DVD the previous Christmas and it was one of my most prized possessions.

Annie and I had been working our way through the series over the last few weeks, and we now found ourselves on the episode where Carrie gets mad at her boyfriend, Aidan, for never wanting to go out on the town. Deeply engrossed, I found myself laughing. "God, Josh and I had this fight all the time. That boy would not leave the house for an entire weekend and be perfectly happy about it."

There was silence for a moment, as I realized what I had said. I hadn't talked about, or even really thought about, Josh in that way in so long. When was the last time I thought about him without desperation and pain? When was the last time I had told a story about him, or remembered something about him, in a completely casual and fond way? I had no idea.

"Ginny." I didn't like the tone of Annie's voice. "Why haven't you called him yet?"

"I can't, Ann," I said flatly.

"I don't understand," she said, picking up the remote to turn down the volume. "Josh isn't just some random bastard that doesn't deserve to know—I mean, he's totally an ass, dumping you and everything. But you guys were really in love." I closed my eyes. She didn't have to remind me of that. "I mean, not like some first-love, crush thing that most of us had in high school. You really, actually, loved him. Right?"

"Yeah," I said quietly. "I really, actually did. And he's not an ass, Ann. I know I let you guys think that, but really, he isn't."

"What do you mean?"

"Things got bad, that last year of school. It wasn't all his fault, honest. He was... he was always good to me." Thinking about Josh like this was physically painful, but it was important to me that she not think he was just some jerk guy.

"Virginia McKensie," she said sternly, "he came here, after dumping you, and slept with you, even though he had no intention of getting back with you. Right?"

"It's not that simple." How could I make her get it? "He loved me, Ann. The break-up was just as hard for him as it was for me."

"Well, if he's actually this good guy, then I *really* don't understand why you can't tell him."

I didn't answer, and eventually Annie turned the volume of the TV back up. Lost in my thoughts, I couldn't concentrate on the show anymore. How could I explain it to her? To make her understand I would have to tell her everything, tell her what I had done.

Tell her how Josh had felt about me in the end, and why. I had never told anyone. And I wasn't ready to start now.

Chapter Seven

Thirteen Weeks: *At last!! You are now out of the dreaded first trimester. You'll be feeling much better in no time! Right now your baby is developing at a phenomenal rate and actually looks very much like he or she will at birth—just a much tinier version! Eyes, nose, mouth, even tiny elbows have formed at this point. As for Mommy, you're probably feeling great as morning sickness decreases, energy increases, and your adorable baby bump becomes more prominent. Aren't you cute? While you may still fit in your baggier regular clothes, use this time as an excuse to go shopping with some girlfriends for your brand new fabulous maternity wardrobe!*—Dr. Rebecca Carr, *A Gal's Guide to a Fabulous First Pregnancy!*

"I refuse to wear this," I told Annie firmly, pushing the offending garment back at her.

"Why not?" she asked. "I think it's cute!"

"Annie, it's practically a muumuu!" I said. And I wasn't exaggerating: voluminous, shapeless, and covered in orange flowers, it was one of the most disgusting pieces of clothing I had ever seen.

"Well what did you expect? It's maternity clothes, not Michael Kors' spring line."

"Annie, Gin is right, that thing is hideous and you know it. If you're not going to be helpful, go look at shoes." Jen briskly put the muumuu back on the rack and steered me over to where she had been looking. It was late January and the three of us were shopping at a consignment maternity shop. Have you ever heard anything more depressing? They couldn't even give it a cute name to hide the depressingness—it was literally called the Consignment Maternity Shop. Gag.

"Cheer up!" Jen chided me. "There's some cute stuff in here!"

I looked at her levelly. "You have got to be kidding me."

"Ginny, you have entirely the wrong attitude about this. We shop at vintage and resale shops all the time. Isn't your favorite jacket that corduroy blazer we found at that resale place in Royal Oak?"

"Yeah, but that jacket was BCBG! It's designer, it was a great find! This place is totally different."

"How do you know?" she asked. "You're not even trying. Look at this the same way you would any other clearance sale you've ever shopped. You love challenges when it comes to shopping!"

I grudgingly admitted that she had a point. I was, in fact, quite an expert at finding the diamond in the rough when it came to fashion. In addition to my BCBG jacket, I was the proud owner of a Diane von Furstenberg wrap dress, a DKNY cashmere cardigan, and, the *pièce de résistance*, a pair of Manolo Blahnik high heel sandals. I would not have been able to afford any of these things at retail prices, but hard work at trunk shows and good luck at resale stores had been my fashion allies for years.

It wasn't like I had much choice, anyhow. My waistline was expanding at an alarming rate, much faster than my baby book (which I had finally started to read—or rather, to skim) warned would happen. I had been getting by okay so far on baggier clothes, but I had never owned many of those. I had always felt that jeans should be tight and skirts even tighter—my legs were my favorite assets, and I was a member of the "play it up" school of thought. My collection of yoga pants and baggy shirts could only be stretched so far, so it was definitely imperative that I walked away from here with some clothes. But was it too much to ask that they be at least somewhat cute?

"Here, try this," Jen said, pushing something at me as she continued to rifle through the racks. "And these too..."

I decided to follow her lead, so I started seriously looking through the clothing on offer. Even Annie seemed to get into it, returning with several pieces that had potential. Once we had a large pile, I found a dressing room and got to work.

I was surprised to find that many of the outfits we had cobbled together were, in fact, pretty cute. Some accentuated the growing baby bump, but in a nice sort of way, while others minimized and disguised it. Soon, I was feeling that familiar rush I got when clothes shopping, the thrill of finding good deals. I was even persuaded to come out and model some things for the girls.

While I had been in the dressing room, Annie had taken it upon herself to find the most hideous pieces the store had to offer. She met me in front of the mirror wearing that first disgusting flowered muumuu. "Are you sure you don't want to change your mind about this one?" she asked seriously. I couldn't help laughing. It really was one of the worst things I had ever seen and it looked even more heinous on, if that was possible.

For the rest of the afternoon, every serious, cute outfit I came out to model was met by one of the girls in something ridiculous. There were plaid stretchy pants, orange knit dresses, and ginormous, polka-dotted, shapeless blouses. We were quickly in hysterics as each girl tried to top the last outfit.

"This one has shoulder pads!" Annie squealed, as she appeared in a neon green silk blouse.

"Stop!" I begged, holding onto Jen for support as I laughed. "You can't make me pee my pants at the Consignment Maternity Shop!"

"She's right, Ann," Jen gasped. "This place is far too classy for peeing your pants!" That, of course, set us right off laughing again.

It wasn't lost on me that I was having fun—actually, I was having a fabulous time. I hadn't been able to say that since finding out about the pregnancy. I looked at my friends, happy and flushed, helping me to get through an afternoon that would have been otherwise unbearable, and I began to wonder if it might be possible to do this after all.

*　　*　　*

We left the consignment shop laden with three bulging bags of fairly cute, and very cheap, maternity clothes. We had left the silly pieces behind, though Annie had made a final push for me to take the flowered muumuu for its comedy value. The girls insisted on taking me out to lunch when we finished. I had worked an extra weekend night the previous week so I would have some cash for the clothes, but they knew money was only getting tighter for me.

I demanded we go to a diner for lunch—though so many foods were making me sick, greasy fried things never lost their appeal. As we waited for our food, I rubbed my belly. "Those baby books are full of crap," I muttered. "Everything says I'm supposed to start feeling better now, but I still feel awful."

"My cousin had morning sickness until she was eight months pregnant," Annie said, taking a slurp of her pop. "Maybe you'll be like her."

I glared at her.

"You've only just started your second trimester," Jen soothed. "Give yourself some time."

Suddenly, I felt a wave of tiredness wash over me. What had I been thinking? One fun afternoon with my girlfriends and magically I thought things would be fine? How stupid could you get?

"You okay?" Annie asked.

I shook my head, afraid I would start crying if I tried to talk.

"Ginny, it's going to be okay," Jen said, reaching across the table for my hand. "I know you don't want to hear this, but I think you'll feel a lot better about things if you sit down and look at your options. I've been doing some research and there are programs that can help you with the expenses of the baby. Why don't you sit down with me when we get home and we can take a look."

I nodded, wiping at my eyes, trying to keep the tears at bay. "It's just...it's just a lot to deal with. And I really, really miss Josh." My voice broke on his name, and the tears were definitely leaking out now.

"You need to call him," Jen said. "It's getting ridiculous that you've waited this long."

The waitress saved me from having to answer, showing up with our food at that moment. She looked at me strangely, but didn't say anything about the tears. After she left, Jen started again. "Ginny, come on. What's the worst thing that could happen? He's going to find out sooner or later, and he's only gonna be more pissed the longer you wait."

I cleared my throat. "There are things you guys don't know, stuff I never told you— about the break-up, I mean. I just...I just need some more time. Please, please try to understand."

Annie looked at me closely. I knew she was thinking about our discussion during *Sex and the City*. "Okay," she said finally. "We'll give you some more time. Come on, you need to eat."

Quietly, we started on our lunch. I couldn't have felt any more different from the way I had felt earlier in the dressing room. All the happiness and calm was gone, and I was left feeling as scared, and as lonely, as ever.

Chapter Eight

From the night of Amanda Doweger's fateful party on, my entire world became Josh. We were already in most of the same classes and Annie, Jen, and my other friends promptly made room for him at our lunch table. I was so pleased to see how well he fit in with our group.

Josh was quiet—or at least, more quiet than me. So much of my life before him had been *loud:* music, parties, laughter. I still loved those things, but I knew I used them, too often, to cover up the loneliness, the silence that had been the mainstays of my childhood. Josh saw me in a way that was different than anyone else. He saw through my bullshit and gave me the ability to be different, to be real, even if only when we were alone. With Josh, for the first time, I could be quiet. I could be still.

My parents disapproved, which I found hilarious. To them, Josh was too artsy, too hippie. I tried to point out that he was the first boyfriend I ever had that respected me, that didn't expect me to put out, but that mattered less to them than his image.

Josh's parents, on the other hand, absolutely hated me. They knew my reputation, they could see what everyone else could see, and they did not think I was worthy of their son.

There was a time when I would have agreed with them, a time I would have characterized myself as unworthy of someone as amazing as Josh. But the crazy thing about being with Josh was that I started to see myself through his eyes. He adored me, and I respected his opinion enough to feel really and truly good about myself for the first time in my life. To Josh I was vibrant, caring, funny, sexy, intelligent, intuitive. To me, he was everything.

We were inseparable through high school. I pulled him along to my parties, to my friends' houses, to dances. Because he was with me, he enjoyed himself, he came out of his shell. As his personality came out, his sense of humor, my friends soon accepted him for him, and not just as my boyfriend—and I was so happy.

Because Josh wrote for the school's creative writing magazine, I joined the staff as well. I had always loved to read and write fiction, but outside of my writing classes I had never been comfortable sharing my work with people. But the fear of judgment could never compete with the feeling of Josh sitting next to me, encouraging and praising me. I loved working on the magazine, I loved the friends I made there. Mostly I loved the feeling of fierce pride it would give me to see how the people there regarded Josh. He was good, very good, and within the walls of the magazine office, he was revered. And he was mine.

When it was time to choose colleges, I never even considered anywhere but where Josh would be. He got a scholarship to State, and although he would have preferred a smaller liberal arts school, the money was too good to pass up. I, of course, followed him. We got an apartment together, to the very strong objection of both of our parents, and I was in heaven. I pictured that, at State, our life would continue along the same trajectory we had started in high school.

For the first three years, it was exactly the way I imagined it. I went to classes, and when I came home, Josh was there. We made our tiny apartment cozy. Josh hung Christmas tree lights around the ceiling and we filled the space with books and photographs. It felt like us—it felt like the first home I had ever really had.

I joined the track team and made friends with the other girls and some kids in my classes. Josh and I both joined *StateInk,* the college's creative writing magazine. We went to parties, hung out with friends, but always, at the end of the night, it was Josh and me, alone in the space we had created together. We cooked together, spent hours reading in contented silence. We talked for ages about nothing, we listened to music, we made love in our small bed. I felt like my life was complete, and I never wanted it to end.

So when everything started to change, it's no surprise that I didn't handle it very well.

Chapter Nine

Sixteen Weeks: As you move more firmly into your second trimester I hope you are feeling much better. Most women enjoy this stage of pregnancy the most. You'll continue seeing the physical changes in your body, but you'll also more than likely feel more energetic and comfortable. You may even notice an increase in your desire for your husband (wink, wink). Enjoy this time with him, ladies, before a crying newborn starts taking up so much of your time!—Dr. Rebecca Carr, *A Gal's Guide to a Fabulous First Pregnancy!*

I was late for work. Again. Despite what Dr. Rebecca Carr kept assuring me in the baby book, I was no closer to feeling energetic. In fact, I was still having morning sickness most days of the week, and my bladder continued to wake me up throughout the night. Moreover, a constant fog of exhaustion surrounded me, no matter how hard I tried to rouse myself. The grey dreariness of February in Michigan probably wasn't helping matters much.

The other desires she kept hinting at were popping up constantly, but as there was virtually nothing I could do about that (short of watching more Colin

Firth movies than was generally considered healthy), I tried hard to not think about my loneliness.

Snow had fallen the night before, but now it was melting into a slushy grey mess. I finally pulled into the Conrad's driveway and slipped my way up the walk and into the house. I was less than ten minutes late, but I had been ten minutes late the day before, and five the day before that, so my stomach was churning with nerves, as well as the omnipresent nausea.

I was surprised to find the house quiet. Taking my shoes off in the foyer I listened for sounds of morning chaos, but I heard nothing. I walked into the kitchen, and found it empty. Where was everyone? I heard someone clear her throat behind me, and I spun to see Kelsie standing in the doorway. One look at her face and I knew a bad morning was about to get much, much worse.

* * *

Thirty minutes later I was sitting on the couch in our living room. I felt mostly shock, but under that was a rising sense of panic. What the hell was I going to do now? Annie came back from the kitchen with a cup of tea, which she handed to me as she sat down on my left side. "Jen's on her way home," she told me. "She told them she was feeling sick and left."

I nodded numbly, although it didn't seem to matter much either way. What could Jen do? "We'll figure something out," Annie promised, though she sounded less than sure. I picked up the remote and turned on the TV, trying to drown out the ever increasing panic building inside me. Annie sat with me, not saying a word, which I appreciated. Platitudes would probably send me over the edge right then.

Jen arrived shortly later, and Annie turned off the TV so she could fill her in.

"I can't believe it," Jen hissed once Annie had finished the story. "I cannot believe she fired you, just like that."

"It's because of the pregnancy," I said flatly. "I know it is."

Annie gasped. "Did she say that?" she demanded.

"No, she was very careful about how she worded it. But she said..." I swallowed, hard. "She said she wasn't sure if I was the most appropriate person to be around impressionable children."

Annie swore.

It had been awful. The kids were already on their way to school, having been driven by a neighbor. Jill was upstairs. Kelsie wouldn't even let me go up to say goodbye. And the way she had looked at me when she told me...it was a look I had seen countless times before. I had seen it on the faces of teachers, on the faces of other girls as they whispered about me behind their hands, on the face of my own mother. She thought I was a whore. She thought I was bad for her kids.

"She can't get away with this," Jen said. "Firing someone over pregnancy is illegal."

"What am I gonna do?" I asked bitterly. "Sue her? Lawyers aren't exactly in the budget right now. Besides, it's not like the work arrangement was really on the up-and-up to start with." Annie and I had always been paid under the table, meaning the families we sat for didn't report paying us and we, in turn, didn't have to pay taxes.

"She gave her some severance too," Annie told Jen. "Probably trying to cover her ass."

"Well that's good at least," Jen said brightly. "How much did you get?"

"One month's wages," I said flatly. I suppose I should have been was grateful: I could have gotten nothing. But what was I going to do when the month ran out? Jen had finally succeeded in getting me to sit down and make some plans. She had been right: there were several programs I would qualify for to help me with expenses. I probably would have been okay if I would have been able to work until the baby came. But now...

"Okay, so we readjust the plan," Jen said firmly. "You have a month to find a job. You have a college degree; you're going to be able to find something. It doesn't have to be perfect; it just needs to be some income."

I looked at her, surprised again at her ability to smooth things over for me, to take control of a situation and make it make sense for me. Jen had never been the most forceful of the three of us. I wondered what else had changed in the years I had been so caught up in Josh.

"We'll put your resume up online. I'll help you." Annie said. "You've always wanted out of that job anyhow. Well, now you are."

"But I'm *pregnant,*" I moaned. "I'm about to become a single mother and I don't have a job. It would have been hard enough to raise this baby alone. How on earth am I going to do it if I'm unemployed?"

"Hang on a second," Annie said, holding up her hand. "What's this crap about you raising the baby alone?"

I stared at her. "Annie, Josh dumped me. I can't even get the courage up to call him. I'd say that's pretty much the definition of alone."

"I'm not talking about Josh," she said, waving her hand dismissively. "I'm talking about us. *We're* going to help you raise the baby."

"Duh. She knows that, Annie." Jen scoffed.

But Annie was looking at me closely. "I'm not so sure she does," she murmured.

"Ginny, don't be ridiculous. Of course we're helping you!"

I felt tears start to well in my eyes. "I didn't want to assume anything..."

"Ginny, we're all going to stay here together once the baby comes," Jen said firmly. "We'll help you take care of it for as long as you'll let us. Okay?"

"Yeah. I, for one, am really looking forward to being an auntie," Annie said, nudging me with her elbow and smiling. "I'm going to teach this kid everything I know about music and art. He or she is going to be the coolest pre-schooler on the block."

I felt too overwhelmed to speak, so I just smiled back at them.

"Something good actually happened last week," Jen added, looking distinctly uncomfortable. "I didn't want to tell you before, because I thought, well, because you've been so worried about money, and, well—"

"Jen, spit it out already!" Annie demanded.

"Well, okay. I got a promotion this week... and it comes with a raise. A pretty good one, actually."

"Jen!" I gasped. "That's awesome! Congratulations!" Jen worked at an event planning firm downtown. She absolutely loved her job. A promotion would be a major deal for her. "Why on earth didn't you tell us?"

"I didn't want you to think I was, like, bragging, or rubbing it in, when you've been so worried about things."

I felt horrible that she would think that way, but I didn't know what to say so I just hugged her and congratulated her again.

"But the point is," Jen continued, "that I think it's only fair that I pay some more into rent than before."

"No way!" I said. "Absolutely not. It is not your job to subsidize me."

"I'm actually not offering, Ginny," Jen said flatly. "If you remember, the rental is in my name. I pay the landlord every month. If I choose to not cash your checks for a while, I am perfectly in my right."

My eyes filled with tears again. "I can't let you do that," I whispered. "Jen, I can't."

She rolled her eyes. "Get a grip, Ginny," she said. "Did you not hear everything we just said about helping you raise the baby? The money's not that big a deal, and it's not forever. "

"It is a big deal," I argued, but she cut me off.

"Listen, I didn't want to get all cheesy on you, but you're forcing me. You have no one to blame but yourself for the sappiness I am about to spout, understand?"

I nodded, smiling weakly.

"You're like my sister," Jen continued. "You're family, Ginny. And so is this baby. So I have every intention of doing what I can to help you and the baby get through the rough patches. And there's not much you can do about it. You have to take help from family, right?"

"My family's never been much in the helping line," I muttered.

"Well, we're your family now," Jen said firmly. "And this is how things are going to go in our family. Deal with it."

*   *   *

Over the next few days, I couldn't help but feel somewhat relieved. I had enough money to live off of for a little while, particularly if rent wasn't going to be as much of a concern. I still wasn't happy about Jen's offer, but I decided for once to stop worrying and just accept the help, particularly as there didn't appear to be much I could do about it. And I had to admit: it was really, really nice to not have to go to work.

I found that I felt much better—not just in the morning, but all day long, when I didn't have to wake up so early. After a few good nights' rest, my appetite started increasing, and foods and smells didn't make me so nauseous. The ever-present body aches even started decreasing after a few days. I wasn't sure if it was just my body moving further into the pregnancy, or the increase in sleep, or even the lack of stress. Regardless of the cause, I was feeling better than I had since finding out I was pregnant.

I let myself rest for a few days before I started the job search in earnest. There wasn't much to look at, to be honest. I had the bad luck of becoming an unemployed single mother in the worst recession in Michigan's history. Even fast food places weren't hiring. I turned in a few applications and sent out some query letters, but my efforts pretty much stalled there.

Annie, on the other hand, came home with great news the week after I was so unexpectedly fired. The community theater where she had been doing some production work had offered her a position as a youth educator. The pay was miniscule, but it was a full-time, real life job in theater. She could quit nannying and focus all her energy on the field she loved. I was thrilled for her, but I couldn't help feeling a little bitter. Both of my roommates now had good news on the job front—would I ever get to join them?

But then, to my great surprise, the good luck did not end with Annie and Jen. Two weeks after I was fired I got my first lead: Annie's mom knew a woman who worked at a small independent bookstore. They were about to start looking for a full-time store clerk, and, if I wanted, she would put in a good word for me before the job was posted. I sent her my resume right away and kept my fingers crossed.

I was thrilled, and more than a little surprised, when I got a call from the manager only two days later, asking if I would be interested in coming in for an interview. After setting up the day and time with the man from the book shop, and thanking him profusely for the opportunity, I immediately called Jen at work. She promised to come straight home at six and run through interview questions with me. It was strange to be excited about something work-related. It was certainly not a feeling I had much experience with.

Chapter Ten

The store, Just Books, was housed in an oldish brick building next to a small restaurant in Rochester, a cute little city about twenty minutes away from our house. Inside, the shelves overflowed with books, creating a cozy, cluttered atmosphere. There were several big, cushy chairs spaced throughout the shelves, and a few were filled with people leisurely reading. I fell in love with it immediately, and knew that even if I didn't get the job, it would be a store I would frequent often.

I approached the register, where an older woman with graying hair was reading a well-worn paperback. "Excuse me," I said, causing her to look up. She smiled at me, and I continued. "I'm supposed to meet with Luke at two, for an interview? My name is Ginny McKensie."

"Of course," she said pleasantly. "I'm Beth. I'm friends with Mrs. Duncan."

"Oh, Beth, thank you so much!" She smiled at me.

"No problem at all; Mrs. Duncan has always been very fond of you."

"Well, I appreciate it. I was starting to get a little desperate!"

"Don't mention it. Just one moment." She stood and weaved her way through the shelves toward a back door. I took the opportunity to browse through the display tables nearest me. From what I could see, they had a great selection.

"Ginny?" A male voice came from just next to me, startling me and causing me to drop the book in my hands. I spun in his direction and immediately caught my breath. I was staring at the most gorgeous man I had ever seen in my life.

* * *

Luke Wright looked to be a few years older than me, though it was hard to tell as I immediately started blushing and had to look away each time he caught my gaze on his face. He was very tall, and had dark hair and eyes. He wore black plastic rimmed glasses and a soft grey sweater with jeans. He would look like your typical sensitive book store type, if it wasn't for his athletic build. It had been a long time since I had been attracted to anyone but Josh, but Luke was completely and totally hot.

We were sitting in a small, messy office just off the back of the sales floor. Luke was reading over my resume but any minute I would have to start answering his questions. I tried to gather myself and calm down. Drooling probably wouldn't help my employment chances.

"So, you majored in English and worked on a creative writing magazine at State," he said, looking up at me at last.

I nodded wordlessly. Smooth.

"And what have you been doing since graduation?"

I cleared my throat, which felt ridiculously dry all of a sudden. "I've been working as a nanny in Bloomfield Hills," I said.

"And why did you leave that job?" he asked politely. Jen and I had rehearsed this question several times. Under no circumstances was I supposed to tell him about the pregnancy.

"Um, I got pregnant and the mother I worked for wasn't happy about it," I blurted out, then immediately slammed my hands over my mouth. Oh my God, did I seriously just say that? Out loud?

Luke's surprised face assured me that I had indeed said it out loud. "I'm sorry," I said quickly, trying to get a hold of myself. "I didn't mean to say it like that. I'm pretty nervous."

Luke smiled kindly. "Please don't be nervous. And there's no need to apologize for being pregnant. We do, on occasion, hire people who have had babies before, though we try not to make a habit of it." He smiled again and his eyes flashed. He was teasing me! Somewhere deep inside, my well-practiced, but long-neglected, flirting instincts were firing up. I couldn't help but smile back.

"To tell you the truth, I was very ready to leave that job. Nannying didn't fulfill my creative passions or talents in the slightest."

"And what would those passions be?" he asked, leaning slightly closer over the desk towards me. Was I crazy, or had his voice just dropped a fraction of an inch? Could he be flirting too?

"I love the written word," I answered, also leaning forward slightly. "Reading, writing, you name it. I'll read just about anything you put in front of me. I like all different genres." He nodded, so I continued. "I love your store," I said intensely. "I can really see myself here." I gave him my brightest smile.

He smiled in response. "You know, I think I can see that myself," he said. "And your resume looks pretty good. What kind of hours would you be able to work if I brought you in?" His words were benign, but there was something still flashing in his eyes, something I was responding to without trying.

"I'm pretty much available whenever," I replied, my voice sounding kind of husky in my ears. God, what was I doing? I was totally flirting with this guy, this guy that I wanted desperately to hire me. I was in danger of screwing this up, and I needed this job. I sat up straighter, pulling back from the table a little.

"Good," he said. Was I imaging things, or did he look slightly flustered? "So what we're looking for here is someone to work the floor, primarily," Luke continued, sounding more serious now. "You'd have to assist customers, put out stock, and operate the register. You've done those kinds of things before at your previous jobs, I take it?" he glanced back at my resume.

"Yes, I could definitely handle those duties."

"I'm also looking for someone who might be able to help me with some of the office stuff," he said, gesturing around the cluttered, messy room. "I don't mind telling you, I'm a little overwhelmed here. Ideally, I'm looking for someone who wouldn't mind assisting me with ordering, bookkeeping, that sort of thing. Does that interest you at all?"

I tried to pull my mind away from listing the many ways I would be willing to assist this man.

"That wouldn't be a problem," I replied.

"Great." He smiled and did that eye flashy thing again. My throat was feeling distinctly dry. "Well then, I'd be very happy to offer you this job."

"Really?" I practically squealed. "Mr. Wright, that's wonderful. Thank you so much!"

"It's my pleasure," he smiled. "And please, call me Luke. So, when would you be able to start?"

"Does Monday work for you?" I asked.

"Sure thing. We open at ten, so the morning shift starts at nine thirty. You'll be training with me for the first week, and then we'll see about you taking some shifts on your own. Sound good?"

"It sounds perfect!"

Luke stood—God, he was so tall. And gorgeous. I followed suit, and he led me back to the front of the store. When we reached the front door, he handed me a stack of papers. "These are your employment forms, tax info, that kind of stuff. There's also details in there about your pay and benefits." I felt like an idiot. I hadn't even thought to ask about pay or benefits. Put a hot man in front of me and all thought and reason leave my mind.

Luke held open the door and smiled down at me. He was standing very close to me, and his eyes seemed to burn into mine. I wondered if he knew the effect he was having on me.

"It was great meeting you, Ginny. I'm looking forward to Monday."

"Me too," I stammered, smiling back as I walked past him and out into the cold. My face felt flushed as I hurried to my car. Once I was inside, I immediately pulled out my cell phone. "Jen?" I said a moment later. "I got the job. And I think I'm in love."

Chapter Eleven

For the next few days I felt like I was walking on air. I was so excited about the new job, and about the fact that I was actually sorting my life out—a little bit at a time. Jen and Annie seemed very happy for me, and probably relieved that I was coming out of the doldrums.

The night after the interview, I told them all about Luke and his gorgeousness. Annie was very interested, but Jen looked at me so sternly throughout my story that I finally stopped talking.

"Okay, what's the problem, Jen?" I asked.

"Do you really think it's appropriate to be flirting with your boss?" she asked sniffily. "Particularly when you are pregnant with another guy's baby? Who you haven't even told about the baby, by the way."

"Give her a break," Annie scoffed. "She's allowed to look at other guys!"

"I just don't think it's appropriate," Jen insisted.

"Jen, as you've never been pregnant, let me just fill you in on one little side-effect," I said. "For the last four weeks I've been hornier than I've ever been in my life."

Annie snorted.

"Seriously," I continued. "My hormones are insane right now. And I haven't gotten so much as a pat on the arm from a guy since this baby was made. A saint would have been turned on by this man, what chance did *I* have?"

"I'm sorry. I just don't want you getting hurt."

"I'm not going to get hurt. Of course nothing is going to come from it. He's just gorgeous, and very fun to look at."

"You never know," Annie argued. "Maybe it will be like a fairy tale. You're single, desperate, pregnant. He's gorgeous, successful. He'll sweep you off your feet and save you from yourself."

It was my turn to snort, and Annie pointed a finger at me. "You don't know, I think he might like you. He gave you the job right away, didn't he? You could end up with this guy!"

"I am not going to end up with him," I laughed. "His last name is Wright, for God's sake."

"So what?"

"So, I'm not going to end up with a man whose name, literally, is Mr. Wright. The universe doesn't have a sense of humor that good."

* * *

The Saturday before I was due to start work, my happy bubble burst a little bit. Catherine called.

"Hello, Virginia," she said, her voice as expressionless as ever. "Your father and I haven't heard from you in quite some time. I thought I should call and make sure you're still alive." I sighed. This was already off to a great start.

"Of course I'm fine, Mother," I answered. "I've just been busy lately. How are you? How's Dad?"

"Oh, we're fine, I suppose. Your father's knee has been acting up, and I still have my headaches, of course, but outside of that we're doing well."

This was how it always went when I talked to either of my parents. Formal, stilted, cold small talk. I suppose it was better than the screaming matches that had characterized my adolescence. That was the benefit of putting twelve hundred miles between us—it was much harder to drive each other to yelling when they were in Florida and I was in Detroit.

They had moved shortly after I went away to college. They sold my childhood house and bought a place in Clearwater, several miles from the beach. I had been there only twice. They kept a small condo here in Michigan and came home a few months out of the year. But our contact was drastically limited now. I'm not sure which of us was more relieved.

"How have you been, Virginia?" Catherine asked. "You say you've been busy? With what?" I noted the condescension in her voice, and felt my skin begin to prickle.

My mother had been less than sympathetic when Josh and I broke up. When I moved home after graduation with no grand career, she clearly felt vindicated. For all my swagger throughout my teen years that I was going to be wildly successful and different from her when I grew up, I had turned out to be a broke, single nanny. Not anything like what I had sneeringly promised her all those years ago.

"Well, I actually got a new job this week, Mother," I answered, knowing this would garner no respect. Store clerk was not much up from a nanny in her book.

"Really?" she asked. "What will you be doing?"

I explained about the job.

"That sounds...nice," she replied.

God, she irritated me. Why had she called at all? She couldn't care less about my life. Had she asked about Annie or Jen, or the house? Of course not. She still thought I was so beneath her. Feeling a spiteful stab of rage within me, I decided it was time she really heard what I had been up to lately.

"Something else exciting has happened, Mother," I said as sweetly as I could. "I actually found out several weeks ago that I'm going to have a baby."

There was complete silence on her end of the phone. I felt a surge of vindictive pleasure. "Did you hear me, Mother?" I asked, in that same sweet voice. "I'm pregnant. I'll be having a baby at the end of July."

"Whose is it?" she whispered, her voice shaking. I felt a momentary pang of regret. Of course I shouldn't have told her like that. I always let my anger and irritation get the better of me with her. But she just had to wind me up, didn't she?

"Virgina McKensie," she demanded, her voice steady and firm now, cold. "I asked you a question, young lady. Who is responsible for this...this *bastard*?"

I felt like she had slapped me. I shouldn't be surprised she would use such language—I had heard it all, and much worse, before, back in my wild teen years. She had warned me that sluts ended up unmarried with bastard children. But to hear it now, now when it was real, was an entirely different matter. Any regret I had felt was long gone. Now I only wanted to hurt her, as much as I could.

"I really have no idea whose baby it is," I said casually. "There've been so many men, you see." And with that, I promptly hung up the phone.

Chapter Twelve

Eighteen Weeks: Your little bundle of joy continues to change in big ways! By now your baby is actually able to hear sounds! Many parents enjoy stimulating this new sense of hearing. Take this time to talk to Baby and encourage Daddy to do the same. Many couples also enjoy playing soothing music for Baby. Some studies suggest what Baby hears now will have an effect on his intelligence and emotional well-being for years to come!—Dr. Rebecca Carr, *A Gal's Guide to a Fabulous First Pregnancy!*

I swore a lot over the next few hours. This was a typical side-effect from talking to my mother. In days past, a conversation on par with this one would have led me straight to a bar, or at least the nearest liquor cabinet. Jen assured me that doing so now would have a detrimental effect on the baby (I had been hoping those doctors' warnings were just for show).

Since booze was not available to me, and I could no longer lose myself in a guy, as I may have done pre-Josh, I resorted to food. Food and swearing.

After telling the whole sordid tale to Jen, she took pity on me and started cooking. I had found that with the second trimester, many of the foods that used to set me off were now appetizing once again. I was very happy about this fact as I tucked into a huge plate of Jen's lasagna. I finished that off with a nice bowl of peanut butter ice cream. Unsatisfied by the gorge-fest, I called Annie and asked her to bring home as much chocolate and potato chips as she could manage.

I spent the next hour eating. All the while I ranted at Jen and Annie about my mother. They had heard it all before—it was a sign of the strength of our friendship that they listened so patiently. When I finally started to exhaust myself on the topic, Jen suggested we get out of the house and take a walk. It was still pretty frigid out, but Annie assured me the cold air would chill out my temper.

We headed out into our neighborhood. It was dark now, and the stars above us were unusually bright in the clear sky.

After a few moments Jen broke the silence. "So, have you thought at all about baby names?" she asked.

"Uh, no, not really," I replied, caught somewhat off-guard.

"Seriously?" Annie asked, clearly surprised.

"I guess I haven't given it much thought." I shrugged.

"Well let's think about it!" Annie said excitedly.

"Oh no, let's not. I don't want to talk about that." The truth was, I hadn't thought a whole lot about the baby itself since finding out it was coming. I mean, intellectually, yes, I knew there was going to be a living, real life baby in our house in a matter of months. But every time I tried to picture it, tried to imagine holding it, I would be overwhelmed with images of Josh in my head. I just couldn't deal with that.

"I think it should be a literary name, since you love books so much," Annie said, clearly ignoring my protests.

"Yeah, that's a good idea!" Jen agreed. "What're your favorite books?"

"Um, I don't know...there's too many." I was being evasive, and I knew it, but my friends didn't seem to care.

"You love *Harry Potter*!" Jen said. "You've read those books about a hundred times. Why not pick a name from that?"

"Ooh!" Annie cried. "Name the baby Dumbledore! That would be unique!"

I laughed in spite of myself. "I'm not naming my baby Dumbledore."

"Maybe a book about wizards isn't the best place to find a name," Jen said seriously. "Pick a different book."

I decided to play along—after all, I would have to figure this out sometime. "I really love Jane Austen books," I said. "*Pride and Prejudice, Sense and Sensibility*...there are some great, classic names in those books. Eliza, Eleanor, Charlotte..."

"Pretty!" Jen breathed. "Oh, Ginny, I really like those. I can so picture you with a little Eliza!"

"Okay," Annie said. "But what if it's a boy?"

She was met with silence. Shit. I had never considered that I might have a boy. I was going to be a single girl raising a kid with my two best girl friends—I had to have a girl.

"Nah," Jen said after a while. "It's a girl. I just know it."

* * *

We lasted only a few more blocks out in the cold before taking refuge in our little house. Annie and Jen decided to settle in with a movie, but I made my excuses and headed up to my room. Talking with the girls about baby names had left me with a strange feeling. Somehow the baby seemed more real to me tonight than it had before. More like reality, and less like an *idea*.

With that feeling came another: guilt. Guilt that Josh had no idea what was going on. I had my reasons for chickening out before, more than I had told the girls, but they were right: Josh deserved to know.

I took a deep breath, picked up my phone, and found his name in my contacts. Squeezing my eyes shut tight, I pressed the call button. The phone rang once, twice—and then, with a clicking noise, a recording picked up. It wasn't Josh's voice—it was an operator. *"The cellular customer you are trying to call can no longer be reached at this number. Please try again."*

I felt like I had been punched in the stomach. Josh had changed his cell number? Josh had changed his cell number and not told me. I couldn't reach him. He didn't *want* me to reach him. With rising panic, I stumbled to the bathroom, where I proceeded to puke up all the comfort food I had ingested in the last two hours.

Chapter Thirteen

To me, the word *contentment* could be summed up by one picture, one memory: me and Josh lying on our bed, wrapped around each other, just talking. Whether we were getting ready to sleep, or we had just made love, or we were simply being lazy with books or movies, we were closest when we were simply lying together.

There was one day, one perfect day, about two years ago. We were in our apartment. We had just eaten breakfast and decided to go back to bed. It was raining outside. I was completely comfortable in Josh's arms, absolutely at peace. In those moments, I could tell him anything, any wish or fear or idea, and he would understand me.

"I had a dream last night," he whispered in my ear. I knew from the sound of his voice that he was smiling. More than that, I knew *which* smile he was smiling. Josh had so many different smiles—excited, introspective, amused. The huge smile that would appear on his face for only a second before he broke into a loud, uncontrollable laugh. My favorite was the one I imagined on his face now—the small, half-smile that meant he was thinking of something beautiful.

"What was your dream?" I whispered back.

"We had a baby," he said, chuckling a little. "A tiny little baby with curly hair and your eyes."

I felt my heartbeat quicken. I could see it too, so clearly. Not just a dream, but a premonition of our future. Of course we would have babies together. We were meant to be together all of our lives, a family.

"Where were we?" I asked, trying to imagine the picture more fully.

"Right here in this bed. We were lying just like this. You were reading, and the baby was lying here." He touched his chest lightly, just next to where my head was resting. "It was sleeping. And I was just looking back and forth between you and the baby, and I was so happy. When I woke up, I still felt that happy."

"Was it a boy, or a girl?"

"I'm not sure. It didn't really matter."

I looked up at him, and his smile was bigger now, and so happy. I kissed him, hard, until I had no breath left, then I lay my head back on his shoulder. "So, what were we calling this ungendered dream baby?" I asked lightly.

He laughed. "We weren't calling it anything. We were just laying here, the three of us, together." He was silent for a long time. "You know what, I think it was a boy."

"Really. Why's that?"

"Well, when I try to picture the baby, the name Daniel comes to my mind."

"Daniel, huh?"

"Yeah, he looked like a Dan," Josh said firmly. "Danny."

I closed my eyes. I could see it too. Josh, and me, and our baby. A tiny baby with Josh's hair and my eyes. "Danny," I whispered.

Chapter Fourteen

Twenty Weeks: This stage is one of the most exciting of your entire pregnancy! You will more than likely visit your doctor in the next few weeks. At this visit, he will probably want to do an ultrasound! Just think: in a few days time you will be looking at the first picture of your baby! You will be able to hear the heartbeat and may even find out the gender if you wish!—Dr. Rebecca Carr, *A Gal's Guide to a Fabulous First Pregnancy!*

"Ginny, what is this?" Annie asked as soon as I stepped foot in the door. She was holding a piece of paper in her hand.

"I don't know, Annie," I replied. "Perhaps I'll be able to tell once I actually get inside the house." She stepped back, allowing me to take off my coat and shoes.

I was in a pretty good mood. I was only about two weeks in, but work had been going really well so far. Luke was still causing me to blush with practically every glance. We had flirted a little bit as he trained me at the store, but for the most part he was still firmly eye candy. Very, very gorgeous eye candy.

After hanging up my coat I held out my hand to see what Annie had been holding. "Oh. This is the confirmation for my ultrasound," I said, squinting at the piece of paper on which I had scribbled the appointment information that morning while talking to the receptionist at Dr. Beldkin's office.

"I thought that's what it was," she said irritably. "And it says the ultrasound is tomorrow?"

"Yup. That's what it says." I didn't understand why she was looking at me so exasperatedly.

"And you weren't planning on telling anyone about this?" she demanded.

"I guess it slipped my mind. What's the problem?"

"The problem? Ginny, you haven't asked anyone to go with you!"

"So? I've been to the doctor a bunch of times alone. Why does it matter?" I asked.

"This isn't just a doctor's visit. This is your *ultrasound*. It's a really big deal! You're going to see your baby! One of us should be with you!"

I rolled my eyes and pushed past her into the kitchen. "Annie," I said patiently, taking down a glass and filling it with water. "It really doesn't matter that much to me. Okay? There is no reason one of you should take off work. I'll be fine on my own."

"No," she said firmly. "Nope. Sorry. You don't go to an ultrasound alone. You just don't. I'm coming with you, end of story."

"Oh, come on—"

"Virginia. End of story means end of story. I brought home Chinese food. So shut up and let's go eat."

I did as I was told. I was never one to argue when free Chinese food was involved.

* * *

The next morning, I felt a little sick. I guess I *was* nervous about the whole ultrasound thing. As Annie drove me to the doctor's office, I decided that I was relieved that I had agreed to let her come with me. Doing this alone would have sucked.

"So, have you decided yet?" she asked.

"Decided what?"

"If you're going to find out!" she said, excited. "About the sex of the baby," she clarified, somewhat exasperated, as I continued to look blank.

"Oh," I said, as I realized what she was talking about. "Hmm...I hadn't really thought about it..."

"You're hopeless," she sighed. "How could you not have thought about it?"

"I don't know. It hasn't really seemed important."

"It's totally important!" Annie was shocked. "Don't you want to decide on a name? And pick colors for the bedding and stuff?"

"Umm..."

I didn't know how to explain it to her. It would sound horrible to tell her that those kinds of details, those fun, mommy-to-be details, were the farthest thing from my mind. Those were the things you discussed while you lay awake at night—with the baby's father. Thinking of stuff like that was what you did when you were excited about a baby.

"Ginny, listen to me, okay?" she said quietly, glancing over and meeting my eyes quickly before she turned her attention back to the road. "I get that this isn't the ideal situation. I understand that you didn't plan for it to happen this way."

I should have known she would guess what I was thinking.

"But we're here now," she continued. "You're *having* this baby; it's going to be a real person, a part of our lives. It's okay to be excited. It's okay to start thinking of the baby—not the pregnancy, not the shitty situation surrounding it, but the *baby* itself. 'Cause it's real now, Ginny."

I was silent. She was right, as usual, but it was so much to take in. Saying it was one thing. Believing it, feeling it, was another matter entirely.

"Just think about it, okay?" She finished her little speech and let the silence, and my thoughts, swirl and settle around me.

* * *

Half an hour later I was laying on the exam table, my belly exposed, while a brisk, no-nonsense technician smeared some cold gel around on my skin.

"This is bizarre," Annie muttered. "Your stomach is huge. You're supposed to be the skinny one. How are we even here? It's so surreal."

"How the hell do you think I feel?" I hissed, glaring at her. "Bitch," I added, for good measure, since *she* wasn't the one laying half naked in front of some stranger. The technician, a middle-aged woman who had introduced herself as something like Barbara or Beatrice, glanced at me in a disapproving sort of way. Annie grinned, and winked at me.

"Well," said Barbara/Beatrice. "I'm ready to get started here. This won't hurt or be uncomfortable at all; the worst part is that cold gel."

I suddenly felt terrified and I drew in a shaky breath.

Barbara/Beatrice smiled at me. "I'm going to be looking at some things to see that the baby seems healthy," she continued, more kindly this time, and I decided she wasn't so bad after all. "We'll take some measurements, listen to the heartbeat, and then, if you'd like, we can tell you the baby's sex. We'll take a picture and you'll be all set to go. Sound good?"

"Sure," I whispered, my voice shaking. Annie immediately reached down and grabbed my hand. Barbara/Beatrice put the wand against my stomach, made some adjustments on the monitor, and suddenly the screen burst into life. It mostly looked like static to me, but in the middle was a round black blobby thing, and inside of *that* was a shape—

"There it is," said Barbara/Beatrice softly. "There's your baby. Everything looks really good so far. I'm going to take a few measurements, and if I just turn this up here..." she twisted a dial and the room was filled with a rapid, pulsating sound. "That's your baby's heartbeat," she said, smiling over at me.

"Holy shit," Annie whispered, eyes glued to the screen, obviously freaked out. I felt pretty freaked myself.

It was a weird combination of terror and something else...something like awe.

"I mean...*holy shit*, Ginny."

"I know," I replied, breathless. I squeezed her hand, feeling the need to anchor myself to something, almost like I was afraid the image on the monitor would overwhelm me.

"I can tell you the sex, if you'd like to know," Barbara/Beatrice said. I tore my eyes from the monitor and met Annie's, which were opened wide in the same expression of awe that I could feel in my own. She raised her eyebrows at me.

"Yeah. I mean, yes, please," I said.

"It's a boy. You're having a baby boy."

A feeling like I have never known crashed over me. It was joy, elation, excitement, fear...It was completely overwhelming and I burst into tears, hardly knowing why. Annie bent down and kissed my forehead, laying her cheek on top of mine, and I could feel her tears, hot on my cheek and mixing with my own. "We're having a baby," she whispered. "Oh my God, Ginny, we're having a baby boy."

* * *

One thing that I had always loved about Annie was her ability to get emotional, show people how she felt, and then immediately go right back to normal. With some people, sobbing uncontrollably over an ultrasound image would have made them feel awkward, uncomfortable. Not Annie.

"You know," she said thoughtfully, as she helped me button my blouse after Barbara/Beatrice had left to develop the ultrasound picture. "Your tits are gonna get huge pretty soon."

I rolled my eyes at her. "I think everything's gonna get huge. I can already barely get my big, fat, swollen feet into my only pair of Jimmy Choos."

Annie snorted. "Jimmy Choos, my ass. I know for a fact you bought those knockoff pieces of crap on the internet. They're not even real leather."

I reached out to pull her hair just as the technician came back into the room. She gave us another disapproving look; apparently the bonding moment with Barbara/Beatrice had ended with the ultrasound. She handed me an envelope with my pictures, instructed me to make an appointment for the following month, and nodded me out of the exam room.

"You keep making Barbara think I'm unfit to be a mother," I mock-scolded Annie as we walked to the front desk.

"Who the hell is Barbara?" she asked. "I thought that chick's name was Denise."

It was my turn to snort as we stepped into line behind a shorter woman with a sleek blond bob. The woman turned slightly toward us and her eyes flicked vaguely in our direction, before she turned her attention back to the front—but then recognition seemed to dawn on her and she did a double take. My heart stopped.

It was Mrs. Stanley, Josh's mother. She stared at me, clearly surprised to see me there, a polite smile forming on her face. And then, *oh my God,* her eyes flicked down over my body to my stomach, and she froze.

"Ginny?" she asked, staring at my prominent baby bump. "Is that...are you...?"

I felt like I might hyperventilate. Josh's mom was here, at my *gynecologist* office, for God's sake. And she knew! She knew about the baby! What if she told him? What was I going to tell *her*?

"Oh my God..." Annie said next to me, realization dawning on her.

"Um, I can...I can explain," I stammered.

Mrs. Stanley was still staring at my stomach and I had no idea what to say to her. I cleared my throat once, and then again, and finally she seemed to pull herself together. Not meeting my eyes she gestured toward the waiting room.

"Perhaps we'd better go talk," she said shakily.

I followed her toward a far couch in an empty area of the room. Annie made as if to come with me but I stopped her with a shake of my head. She took a seat near the door, but I could feel her eyes on my back as I walked away from her, and I took some strength from knowing she was there, watching.

I sat down next to Josh's mother, trying desperately to think of what to tell her. I was relieved when she started first. "You're pregnant," she said, more a statement than a question. I nodded my head. "Is it...is it Josh's?"

"Yes," I said quietly, and she closed her eyes swiftly, almost like she was flinching. I felt so bad for her then, so guilty. "I'm sorry."

"Does he know?" she asked.

"No...not yet." I thought I saw relief on her face, but it passed quickly enough that I thought I must have imagined it. "I called him, but his number's changed." The excuse felt flimsy in my ears. "I know I need to tell him, and I will, I just...I just didn't know how."

She nodded her head somewhat distractedly. "How far along are you?" she asked.

"Four months. He's due in July."

Her eyes snapped up, meeting mine for the first time. "He?" she asked sharply.

"Yeah, it's a boy. I just found out, actually."

She seemed, somehow, even more dazed than before.

"Are you going to tell Josh?" I asked.

"Do you want me to?"

"No...no, it should be me," I answered, though the mere thought of telling him made me feel immediately cold all over. "I've been thinking I'd go up to Lansing, because he changed his number... He hasn't called lately—I'd asked him not to actually..." I knew I was babbling and I made a conscious effort to stop talking, but it didn't seem like Mrs. Stanley was really listening to me anyhow.

"He's coming home this weekend," she said slowly. "If you wanted to tell him in person, I could arrange it for you, tell him you need to see him."

"Really?" I was surprised that she was willing to help me. To be honest, I was surprised she hadn't yet started calling me a whore, or slapping me or something. Mrs. Stanley had never quite warmed to me—and that was all before she found out I was knocked up with her son's illegitimate baby.

"What choice do I have?" she asked rather sharply, displaying some anger for the first time. "He should know, and like you said, you should be the one to tell him." Abruptly she pulled out a pen and an envelope from her purse. She scribbled something on the envelope, tore off the piece she'd written on, and handed it to me. "I'll make sure he's at that café at that time. You can tell him then." And before I had a chance to say another word, she got up and swept out of the room.

Chapter Fifteen

Annie called Jen as she drove us home, informing her we were going to need major reinforcements of pizza to get through the night. I was still feeling somewhat shell-shocked. First the ultrasound—the crashing realization that I was having this baby, for real—and then the run-in with Josh's mom. It was a lot to take in for one afternoon.

Jen met us at the house, pizzas and pop in hand, and Annie immediately began filling her in on what had happened. Jen was appropriately shocked.

"Of all the coincidences in the world," she muttered. "Well, I guess now it at least solves that problem for you."

"What problem?"

"Well, trying to figure out when, and how, to tell Josh. She took the choice away from you. Now you know."

"Yeah, but I'm no closer to knowing *how* to tell him." I sighed. This was what I had been avoiding for so long. Just thinking of seeing him again, under any circumstances, made my heart start to beat faster. How was I going to manage to also tell him that his life was going to change?

Annie reached for another slice of pizza. "Do what I do when I'm performing," she advised. "Learn your lines really well so that when the time comes, and you're nervous, you can just jump in without thinking about it. Just do it."

"What are you, a fucking Nike commercial now?"

"Fine, make fun. I'm only trying to be fucking helpful." She stuck her tongue out at me, in the process showing me a mouthful of chewed pizza.

"Oh my God, I'm going to be sick," I moaned.

"Oops, sorry. Forgot I can't do things like that around preggers over here."

"You know what I think?" Jen said, interrupting us both. "I think the two of you swear way too much."

"Okay, *Mom*," I said childishly.

"That's just my point: you're *going* to be a mom. What mom do you know that says the eff-word twenty times a day?"

"The eff-word? What are we, twelve?" I laughed.

"You know, she does have a point," Annie said. "You do have a pretty dirty mouth."

"Me? Are you serious? You swear me under the table!"

"Yes, but I, unlike you, would be willing to curb my swearing for the benefit of little baby Dumbledore," Annie said beatifically.

"I am *not* naming my baby Dumbledore," I growled. "And I think we both know that I could stop swearing before you could."

"Wanna bet?" Annie asked eagerly. "What do you say about a little wager?"

We decided that for every use of the four letter curses we would have to pay each other a dollar. Minor swear words would cost fifty cents. I smiled at Annie broadly. "I have a feeling you're going to be paying for my baby's college education with this bet."

"Or you might be buying me a new Coach handbag," she replied, grabbing the last slice of pizza from the box.

"So when did she arrange for you guys to meet?" Jen asked.

I groaned. "On Saturday morning."

"Want us to come with you?"

"No, I think I should probably do it myself," I sighed. "Thanks though."

After that we decided to stick a movie on in the hopes that it would distract me from what was coming. It worked. Sort of.

*   *   *

I took time getting dressed and ready Saturday morning, choosing my outfit with care and spending far longer than usual blowing out my long brown hair silky straight. As I reapplied eye shadow for the third time—I couldn't seem to get it to smudge in just the right way—I had to admit that I was being pretty silly. What was I expecting? Did I really think any amount of primping would soften the blow of what I was about to tell him? However, I had always felt that looking good was the best weapon (sometimes the only weapon) you had when the chips were down, and I wasn't about to backtrack on that now.

I got to the coffee house early, figuring that if I saw Josh and then had to walk across the room to meet him, my legs just might give way first My palms were sweating like crazy before I even finished stirring my herbal tea. How was I going to get though this? I added a sugar packet and, in doing so, bumped my cup with my shaking hands. "Shit," I muttered. There was a very noticeable yellow stain spreading across the thigh of my khakis. As I dabbed at it furiously with a napkin, I heard someone clear her throat.

I looked up, straight into the eyes of Mrs. Stanley. "What are you doing here?" I blurted out in surprise.

"Good morning, Ginny," she said stiffly. Looking distinctly uncomfortable, she pulled out the chair across from me and sat down, staring determinedly at the table and not meeting my eyes. "Josh isn't coming."

"Why not?" I asked, feeling the beginnings of dread creeping up from my toes. "Did something happen?"

"He didn't want to see you," she answered, still not meeting my eyes. "I told him you had news for him, news he needed to hear, but he refused."

I felt the room begin to spin. Could Josh really feel so apathetic towards me that he wouldn't even see me?

"I felt I had no choice but to tell him about the baby," she said flatly. "I'm sure you'll agree there was nothing else I could have done."

Oh crap. *Crap!* Josh knew! He knew about the baby! But if he knew then why...

"Why isn't he here then? If you told him, why didn't he come?" I asked in bewilderment.

She finally met my eyes then, and hers were full of pity. "He didn't want to see you," she repeated.

I stared at her, completely aghast. What was she saying?

"Josh does not wish to have anything to do with this situation," she said, her voice shaking somewhat. "I'm sure that is hard for you to hear, and I apologize, but there's no point in pretending otherwise."

I couldn't take it in. Was she seriously telling me that Josh wasn't going to...to what? To see the baby? To acknowledge him at all? How could that be possible?

"Josh loved you once," she said, looking down again and staring at her hands. "But things have changed. He just got an amazing job offer at a magazine in Seattle and he'll be moving within the month. He doesn't want anything to tie him down, to tie him here."

The things she was saying to me weren't making sense. I couldn't imagine Josh ever, ever choosing to ignore me if he knew about the baby. And even if he did, surely he would have the balls to come and tell me himself. I opened my mouth to try and ask this question, but no sound came out. My throat was completely dry, my cheeks burning hot.

Seeing that I wasn't going to respond, Mrs. Stanley pressed on. "I know this seems out of character to you, but you must understand. Josh has his entire future ahead of him. He's worked so hard, for so long, and now he's finally getting all the things he's ever wished for."

But that wasn't right. In the list of things he had wished for, I had certainly been high up there at some point. Yes, we had broken up. But Josh had loved me. How could he do this? He would never do this.

"He wouldn't do this," I whispered. "I know he wouldn't. I want to talk to him. Give me his new cell number."

"He asked me not to," she said.

I stared at her in disbelief. "You cannot tell me you agree with this. You can't believe this is the right thing for him to do."

"My son deserves the future he has worked for," she said coldly. "I'm sorry you've gotten yourself into this situation, but you can hardly expect him to give up everything—"

"I got *myself* into this situation?" I asked incredulously. My shock was turning to anger. "I didn't get myself pregnant, Mrs. Stanley. Josh figured prominently, I can assure you."

She narrowed her eyes at me. "Ginny, Josh told us that you were unhappy about the break-up. 'Desperate to get me back' were his words, I think. Do you really expect me to believe that this was completely an accident?"

It was like she had slapped me. Had Josh really told her that?

"Listen, I'm sorry," she said, breathing deeply as if she was trying to calm herself. "I know this isn't easy. And I know that my son has a responsibility. That's why his father and I are prepared to help you financially."

I could only stare at her. Was she out of her mind?

"We want what's best for our son. We also want to make sure his responsibilities are taken care of. We would like to give you child support, beginning now, in the amount of two thousand dollars per month."

"Let me get this straight," I said, my voice thick with bitter amusement. "You want to pay me to stay away from Josh? Do you actually think that I would agree to that?" I laughed bitterly. This lady was out of her mind. But why on earth was Josh going along with this?

Mrs. Stanley sighed. "Ginny, you don't have very much choice. Josh doesn't want to see you. He doesn't want to know this baby. He's moving across the country in a matter of weeks. It's up to you whether you take the money or not, but nothing you can do will make Josh be a part of your life."

"I don't believe you. I don't. If Josh really feels this way he needs to tell me himself."

"He thought that would be too hard for both of you." She sighed and reached into her purse. She pulled out an envelope and what appeared to be a photograph, which she set face down on the table so I couldn't see it. "He wrote you a letter." She handed me the envelope. I stared down at it mutely. Written across the front, in painfully familiar handwriting, was my name.

"I'm sorry about all of this," she said softly. "I really am. But Josh's dad and I support his decision. You need to accept that this is what Josh wants."

"No," I whispered, still staring at the envelope. Josh's handwriting. It couldn't be true. "No. I trust Josh. He loved me. He wouldn't do this."

Slowly, very slowly, she turned over the photograph. It was Josh, his arms around another girl. She was short and had blonde pixie hair. Josh was laughing toward the camera, and she was smiling up at him. I realized with dread that I knew her.

"I didn't want to show you this but...that's Amy. They've been together a few months. It's all happened so fast, falling in love and all that..." She met my eyes and spoke with a firm, emotionless voice. "She's moving to Seattle with him. They're engaged, Ginny."

Chapter Sixteen

My life with Josh was perfect for a long time. I know people use the word *perfect* too lightly, but this really was. Yes, we were usually pretty broke, and sure, we fought sometimes, but there literally wasn't a thing I would have changed about our relationship.

Early in our senior year of college, a few things happened. At the time, they didn't seem like such a big deal. First of all, Josh was chosen to be the editor of *StateInk,* the creative writing magazine the two of us worked on. I was thrilled for him, and he was over the moon. The job required a lot of his time and soon he was home less and less. I missed him. I tried to stay busy, to keep my mind off his absences, but it was hard. I hated going out without him, trying to be social, trying to have fun on my own. Without Josh at my side, I was picking up some of my old habits—I was partying too much, staying out too late. It wasn't long before I noticed my drinking was increasing, a lot.

Josh started noticing too, and I knew he didn't approve. There was this one night, this awful night, that I remember so clearly. Josh had a deadline, so he and some staff were staying late to finish the layout. We had planned to go to a house party with some friends of mine from the track team. I was sad he had to cancel, and a little pissed, to be honest. He promised he would meet me as soon as he could, so I went alone.

I tried to have fun with my friends. It was sort of a strange mix of people, different from who Josh and I normally spent time with. There were a lot of jocks there, and some boys you just knew were from frats. A lot of people were smoking pot, and the beer drinking was progressing very quickly for so early in the night.

I was on my fourth beer, and just starting to get a buzz, when he approached me. I don't remember his name (I'm not sure if I ever knew it) but I do know he was on the lacrosse team. Or maybe it was hockey. Regardless, he sat down next to me on the couch, sitting way closer than was necessary. He flattered me, told me I was hot and he had been watching me all night. To me, he was nothing. Not particularly cute, not particularly smart or funny. But he was paying attention to me, and that felt good.

I had no intention of doing anything—of course I would never do anything. But I didn't get up and move, either. Instead, I kept drinking while he kept flirting, and when he pulled out a joint, I had some of that too.

Some of my friends joined us, and everything anyone said seemed hilarious to me. I remember laughing a lot, loud and obnoxious, and leaning up against the guy. And then I looked up and Josh was standing there, across the room, watching me.

He didn't seem angry, or jealous. He was just watching me. But I saw something in his eyes I had never seen before. He wasn't looking at me like he normally did, like I was special. He wasn't looking at me like I was pretty, or smart, or someone to be proud of. He was looking at me like I was a drunk, loud, obnoxious slut at a party.

*   *   *

Josh never said anything to me about that night, but things felt different to me after that. It was hard to shake the memory of how he had looked at me. Sometimes, when I closed my eyes, it was right there behind my eyelids, clear as could be. If Josh was gone when the memory would hit me, I would try to erase it with booze, or the noise of a party, or the attention of other people. Sometimes it would hit me when we were together, and I had to work very hard to remind myself that he loved me.

In December, Josh got really surprising news: he had unexpectedly won a scholarship to live and study in London for two months in spring semester. I was thrilled for him. Slightly jealous, and definitely worried sick about being apart, but thrilled for him all the same. It was an amazing opportunity, an affirmation of his talent and hard work.

The night he got the news, we decided to go out and celebrate with some friends from the magazine. Josh picked a Mexican restaurant close to campus, and the rest of us spent several hours complaining about our massive jealousy. I teased him along with everyone else, though the more we discussed it, the larger the pit of fear in my stomach grew.

"I just knew you'd get it," Amy, a pixie-looking little sophomore, sighed as we moved onto our third round of margaritas. Amy had always struck me as rather shy, but it was obvious to me that she harbored a major crush on her editor. I had never given it much thought, secure as I was in my standing with Josh. In fact, I had always thought it was kind of cute, the way she would blush when he spoke to her directly. Tonight though, she was getting on my nerves. The more she drank, the bolder she became, gushing over Josh and staring at him with naked adoration.

"I mean, when they turned you down back in September, I was so shocked!"

Her words took a second to sink in. He first applied in *September*? Why didn't I know anything about this?

"It might seem lucky that the other guy backed out, but you totally deserved it more in the first place!"

I felt my stomach clenching. What was going on here? Josh had made it sound like the scholarship opportunity came totally out of the blue. If he had applied, and been rejected, back in September, why was this the first I had ever heard about it? Surely there was some kind of misunderstanding—but Josh gave himself away. With one quick little worried glance in my direction, I got it. He hadn't told me on purpose, and he knew I had good reason to be upset about it.

I didn't say much the rest of the evening. Any sense of celebration had left me entirely, replaced by a feeling of dread. Josh and I talked about everything. I mean, *everything.* Why would he have chosen to keep this from me? I was relieved when the dinner was over, but at the same time I was not looking forward to going home.

Our ride home on the bus was quiet. I didn't want to fight with Josh—not when he had so much to celebrate. I didn't want to ruin the night for him. But I also couldn't shake the sense that something bad was happening here, happening to us.

"Ginny," he said, breaking the silence. "I'm sorry. I should have told you I was applying."

"Why didn't you?"

Josh sighed. "I was worried you'd take it badly. I was worried you'd be upset and spend the next five months miserable, dreading me leaving."

I was stunned. Did he really think of me that way? In his eyes, was I some needy, dependant clinger? Did he really think that I would worry more about what I was losing than what he was gaining?

"I wouldn't have been like that," I said, my voice small. "When you told me this afternoon, I was so happy for you."

He was quiet for a moment. "You haven't been acting that happy since I was named editor," he burst out, startling me. He sounded pissed.

"What are you talking about?"

"Ginny, give me a break. I see how you've been. Annoyed when I work late, partying all the time. What, are you trying to make me jealous?"

"Make you jealous? Are you kidding me?" I was getting pissed too. Where was he getting this from?

"I've just been trying to keep busy, since you're never around!"

"Do you hear yourself?" he asked. "Do you have any idea how much pressure that puts on me? Something good happens to me and you have to work to stay busy. That, that right there, is our problem."

"I wasn't aware that we had a problem," I said, my voice shaking. I tried to remind myself that Josh had been drinking, that he would never sound this cruel otherwise.

"Ginny..." Josh trailed off. I felt panic well up inside me. "Let's talk about his when we get home." He took my hand, calming me somewhat. We sat like that, silent, holding hands, until our stop.

When we got to our apartment, Josh took me into his arms before I had a chance to take off my coat. "I'm sorry," he whispered against my hair. "I should have told you in September, and I shouldn't have gotten upset with you just now. You haven't done anything wrong."

I held onto him tightly, willing myself to believe that things were going to be okay. "Let's lay down," he said, releasing me. "We can talk in bed."

In the darkness, wrapped in our blankets, he stroked my hair. "Ginny, what I should have said is...I worry about you."

"Why?" I asked.

"Sometimes it seems like you rely on me too much." He sounded uncomfortable.

"I rely on you because I love you," I said, hurt. "You're everything to me...I thought you felt the same way."

"I do! Ginny, you know I do." He sighed. "I just worry, because when something happens that doesn't involve both of us, I feel like you don't have anywhere else to go. You don't have a back-up. And then you revert back to..."

"Crazy-party-slut-girl?" I asked.

He chuckled. "You have never been a slut. Crazy party girl, maybe. And there's nothing wrong with that. I just think you bury yourself in it. You always did. When you're not happy you hide in that crap."

I was quiet. Josh was right. It was what I had always done.

"I just wish you could find something that made you happy, totally independent of me."

I thought about that for a long time after Josh had drifted off. What on earth could ever make me happy besides him? And, despite what he had said, I felt very, very worried. This had been on his mind for a long time, and he had never told me. What else was he thinking about me?

Chapter Seventeen

When I got home from the coffee house I went straight to my room, ignoring Annie and Jen's protests and questions and slamming the door in their faces. I sat on my bed for a long time, staring at the envelope. I couldn't bring myself to open it.

How could this have happened? How could Josh have done this to me? I could maybe, someday, accept the fact that he didn't love me anymore. But I could not believe that he could ever, ever treat me so cruelly. Not after all we had been through together. But the proof of his actions was sitting in my hands.

After a while, Annie managed to get my cheap bedroom lock undone using a nail file. She and Jen burst into the room and demanded to know what happened.

"He didn't show up," I whispered. My voice sounded hoarse, like I had been screaming. Only then did I realize that tears were streaming down my face and the weird noise I had been hearing was my own sobs. "His mom came instead." I tried to wipe my eyes, to pull myself together.

"What do you mean?" Jen asked, confused. "He doesn't know?"

"He knows. She told him."

"I don't understand..." Jen began. I cut her off by handing her the letter.

"He wrote this for her to give to me. He knows, but he didn't want to see me." I looked up at them. Jen looked pale, her eyes wide. Annie seemed merely confused. "You can read it, if you want. I couldn't do it."

Annie pulled the envelope from Jen's hand and ripped it open. "Hey, there's a ton of money in here!" she said.

"It's from his parents."

"Why are his parents giving you cash?"

"Just read the letter, Annie."

She pulled out a piece of paper. As she read, her eyes narrowed. "You bastard," she hissed.

"What? What does it say?" Jen demanded.

"You can read it out loud, Annie. I don't care," I said. Maybe something in it would make sense to me, help me understand.

" 'Dear Ginny,' " she read. " 'I am so sorry to tell you like this, but I could not come and see you today. I think it would have been too painful for both of us. It also would have been painful for Amy, my fiancé.

I take full responsibility for our past mistakes. I hope that you agree to take the money my parents have offered: it's the least we can do. But I have another responsibility now, one to Amy, and to myself. I need to go to Seattle, start fresh. Being a part of all of this would make that impossible. I'm so sorry. I hope you can understand someday. I wish you nothing but the best, and I hope you will be happy. Goodbye.' "

Jen sank down on the bed next to me, looking stunned. "I can't believe this," she said shakily.

Annie was slowly refolding the letter and putting it back in the envelope with the cash. When she finished, she looked up at me, and I was truly afraid of what was in her eyes. "I am going to kill him," she said flatly. "I swear to God, Ginny, I'm going to drive there right this second and kick his coward ass."

"What good would that do?" I asked bleakly.

"It would make me feel better!" she cried.

"I don't even know where he lives now," I whispered. "Our lease expired in January. He could be anywhere now. And I don't even have his number."

"Who the hell is Amy?" Annie asked.

"She was on the magazine with us. His mom had a picture of them together." I swallowed, hard. "His mom had a picture of her...she said...she said they're engaged. She's moving to Seattle with him..."

The reality of what was happening crashed over me like a wave. Josh was gone, really gone, forever. He didn't love me. He didn't want me or our baby boy. He was going to marry someone else. "Oh my God," I whispered. "Oh my God, oh my God..." I started crying again, huge racking sobs that shook my entire body. Jen grabbed me in a hug and held on tight.

It felt like the walls were falling in around me. Everything that happened up until this point—the break-up, the baby, losing my job, feeling so afraid— was nothing compared to this. Nothing at all. To lose Josh, to really lose him forever, was more than I could stand.

I don't know how long I cried like that. In my head I was seeing pictures of me and Josh, like a film reel. Every happy moment we had had. So many times when he had looked at me, smiled at me, kissed me. That love was gone now. He was giving it to someone else and I was alone. Alone with our baby, who Josh didn't even want to know.

Jen and Annie lay in my bed with me, holding me and stroking my hair, trying to wipe my eyes and calm me down. Mostly, they just let me cry.

After a while (an hour? more?) my tears started to subside and Jen persuaded me to sit up. "You should take a shower," Annie said gently. "You'll feel better." I looked at her and numbly noticed that her eyes were red-rimmed too, as if she had been crying right along with me.

They helped me into the shower. I felt weak, helpless. I stood under the hot water for a while, slowly washing my make-up off and shampooing my hair. I wrapped myself in my robe and went out to lay on the couch, where I stayed for the rest of the day, staring, unseeing, at the wall.

Jen and Annie were scared for the baby. I could tell from the way they skittered around me, asking what I needed and trying not to let me see how often they stared at me. Jen tried to convince me to eat, but the food turned to sawdust in my mouth and I went to lay down again.

It was dark outside now, so I knew it had been hours since I met Mrs. Stanley at the coffee house, but I had little sense of time passing. The entire day was a blur of pain and fear. I felt broken. I knew being so upset, so overwhelmed, was bad for the baby, but I couldn't bring myself to care. All I could think of was Josh. Memories of him had taken over my head and my heart and I couldn't shake them out. I felt feverish and shaky and I wondered if I was having some kind of a breakdown.

And then, out of nowhere, the baby moved.

It was an indescribable feeling. It felt almost as if there were a butterfly in my belly, gently nudging me from the inside. I had never felt anything like it. It was amazing.

I sat up slowly on the couch, my mouth hanging open and my hands drifting down to my belly. Jen looked up from the book she was reading in the recliner. When she saw the look on my face she stood up quickly and came towards me. "What? What's wrong, Ginny?" she asked worriedly.

"Nothing," I murmured. "Just...just wait." The fluttering had stopped so I stayed perfectly still, willing it to start again. And then—"Oh!" He moved again. I let out a shaky breath, closing my eyes. "Hello!" I whispered, laughing, as I rubbed my stomach. "Hello, baby!"

"Ginny?" Jen asked again, kneeling on the floor before me. "What's going on?"

I opened my eyes, grinning from ear to ear. "Oh, Jen," I said, tears filling my eyes yet again—but these tears were totally different. "He's moving! I can feel him!"

Jen gasped. "The baby?"

I nodded, laughing again. I felt light, happier than I could have believed. "He's moving. I can feel him!" Jen laughed too, her eyes wide. Unable to sit still a minute longer, I reached out and grabbed her, hugging her tight. "It's my baby, Jen!" I said.

I was absolutely in awe. Ten minutes ago I had been deep within the hell of my darkest moments, not caring about anything, including the baby. I hadn't believed I'd be able to get through the rest of the day, let alone the pregnancy.

And then my baby had reached out from inside, shaking up my entire world, pulling me back to life. The pain of Josh hadn't receded, but it had been completely eclipsed by my baby. My baby was *real*. My baby needed me. And I knew, in that moment, that I loved him more than I had ever loved anything else— including his father.

My baby had broken through the pain and rejection I had been living with since July to let me know he needed me. I, in turn, was going to do everything I could to take care of him, to love him. Josh didn't seem to matter so much now. My baby and I were a team.

Chapter Eighteen

Twenty-two Weeks: You're now past the halfway mark! Before you know it, you'll be welcoming your baby into the world! If you haven't already, you'll more than likely feel the baby begin to move sometime in the next few weeks. You also will notice that a lot of growth is happening in your belly area! If you didn't have a noticeable baby bump before, you probably will soon! In the next few weeks you will have gained anywhere from ten to twenty pounds. Make sure you keep eating healthy. Don't use the baby as an excuse to pig out!—Dr. Rebecca Carr, *A Gal's Guide to a Fabulous First Pregnancy!*

"Wow!" Annie said from the doorway to the kitchen, startling me as I searched for a clean juice glass in the cabinet.

"What?" I asked, looking over at her.

"You look really pregnant today. Like, really, *really* pregnant."

I looked down at my stomach. I was wearing a blue sweater shift dress over grey leggings. I had been trying to avoid tops with an empire waist because I thought they over-emphasized the bump. This dress was designed to hang straight down from the neckline,

113

but the cashmere was, admittedly, pretty strained over my belly.

I sighed. "Yeah, everything is fitting me like this lately. It seems like my stomach suddenly popped out over night."

Annie was still staring at my middle. "It's weird," she finally said.

"Gee, thanks, Ann," I muttered, pouring myself some orange juice.

"Sorry. I mean, you totally look cute, it's just strange. Like you said, it seems like it happened overnight."

"Right?" I asked. "I've been feeling like a fatty for ages, but now it looks more preggers, and less chubby, ya know what I mean?"

"The dress is cute," she said. "Did you get that at the maternity place?"

"No, it's actually just plus size. From Macy's."

Annie laughed. "You got paid last week, didn't you?"

"I did indeed! First paycheck." I couldn't help smiling. It had felt great to earn that check. It had been a while since I had gotten a legitimate check from a business, rather than under-the-counter babysitting money. It wasn't great pay, but it did come with insurance. Plus, I loved working at the book store. Really, really loved it.

"I have to say, it's nice to see you getting dressed up," Annie said, joining me at the kitchen table. "When you were nannying it got pretty depressing to see you in yoga pants and sweats every day."

She had a point about that. When I was nannying, I was unhappy. Unhappy about Josh, unhappy about my job. Those feelings were totally reflected in how I dressed. Which was kind of sad, if you think about it. I was a fashion girl, always had been. I loved doing my hair, putting on make-up, trying to look cute. I shouldn't have let anyone change that about me.

"I'm feeling better," I said to Annie. "When I feel good, I like to look good."

She smiled. "Well, I'm happy to see it."

* * *

As I drove to work a few minutes later, I thought about my conversation with Annie. It was very true, what I had told her. I was feeling much better these days. Work helped. Like I said, I enjoyed it. I got to spend my days talking with customers about books— what could be better than that? I also enjoyed the office work I was doing for Luke. It was calming for me to sit in front of a sheet of orders, making sense of the numbers, creating order from chaos.

The people I worked with were great. In addition to Luke—who, I had discovered, was funny and nice, as well as hot—there was Beth, the friend of Annie's mom who had helped me get the interview. Beth was very sweet. She spent every minute she wasn't with a customer reading well-worn romance paperbacks. She had worked as a librarian for years—you could tell she adored books just by looking at her.

There was also Jack, a skinny college-aged kid with bad acne. Jack was pretty quiet and kept to himself for the most part, but he was always polite when our paths crossed. There were a few other staff who worked nights and weekends, but our schedules rarely overlapped.

Work wasn't the only thing making me happy these days. Since the day I had felt the baby move, I had been almost delirious with happiness every time I thought about him. My extreme indifference prior to the ultrasound had completely melted away—now I couldn't wait for this baby to be born.

Shortly after the baby had moved, I made up my mind that Josh was off-limits. I wouldn't let anyone mention his name and I wouldn't let myself think about him. Or, at least, I tried not to. The baby helped. I knew this kid was going to be the most amazing little guy ever to be born. If Josh didn't want to be a part of that, he clearly wasn't worth my thoughts.

I got to work a few minutes early. That was another thing: I was sleeping better, and waking up for a nine thirty job was so much easier than the seven a.m. start time at the Conrad's. Plus, waking up for something I actually enjoyed made me happy and gave me energy.

The store front was empty when I walked into Just Books. Luke had been pleased enough with my training that he no longer needed to be at the store with me all the time. Usually I split my shifts pretty evenly with him and Beth, who was supposed to be in today. Jack would show up in the afternoon, when we would usually be a little busier. But, so far, I appeared to be the only one here.

"Beth?" I called, heading back towards the stock room.

"Hey, Ginny, I'm in here," yelled a voice from the office. It was Luke.

"What are you doing here?" I asked, walking into the office. Luke was sitting at the desk, rustling through papers in an irritated sort of way.

"Beth called in," he answered, his voice somewhat curt. "Her grandson is sick or something."

"That's a bummer," I said, leaning against the desk. "Did you have plans today?"

"Yeah," he sighed. "But duty calls." I couldn't help but note the bitterness in his voice. I had often wondered why Luke owned this place. He seemed to enjoy talking with customers and recommending books to them—but he clearly detested the business aspect of running the store, and there were days he seemed to resent being there.

"Oh well," he sighed, more mildly, as he turned towards me and smiled. As he looked at me, I noticed a small raise of his eyebrows behind his glasses. "Wow," he said. "You look great today!"

I felt a rush of warm pleasure shoot through me. Luke's compliments always seemed so genuine. "Thanks," I said. "I did a little shopping with my first paycheck."

He laughed as he stood up, leading me out towards the store. "I'm glad to hear it," he said.

We got to work cleaning up the store, restocking books from last night and putting away a new order. As we worked, we chatted comfortably. Josh had lent me the first book in a Stieg Larsson series, and we had differing opinions on it. He was trying to convince me to continue on to the sequel but I was refusing.

"How can you judge something when you've only read one third of it?" he challenged.

"There are too many wonderful things to read to waste time on something I don't like," I responded.

Luke snorted. "What a limiting viewpoint."

I shrugged. "I'm a busy lady."

"Fine. What are you going to read instead that's so much better?" he demanded.

I smiled at him dreamily. "*Sense and Sensibility*."

"Oh my God, you have got to be kidding me," he said.

"Nope, I'm going to read *Sense and Sensibility* for the twentieth time. And it will be heavenly."

He merely rolled his eyes at me.

"What, you don't like Austen?"

"No, I don't like Austen. I don't like books about girls who obsess about marrying rich men."

I stopped what I was doing to glare at him. "You clearly had no understanding of what you were reading."

"Oh, someone is defensive about her favorite author!" he laughed.

"You bet your ass I am," I replied. "How many Jane Austen books have you read, anyhow?" I asked.

"Um...one?" he answered. I laughed.

"Seriously? You're going to judge something when you've read less than one *sixth* of it?" It was Luke's turn to laugh. "Austen was a social commentator. Yes, she wrote about the need for women of that day to find security with men, but she also wrote women who were strong enough to refuse to settle for less than true love, even when they were poor. She was brave and visionary, and men with such a 'limiting viewpoint' should read before they judge."

"Okay, okay!" Luke held up his hands in surrender. "How about I read Jane Austen and you agree to finish the Larsson trilogy?'

I smiled, and held out my hand for him to shake. "Deal."

Chapter Nineteen

The rest of the day continued along the same lines. It was slow in the store, and Luke seemed in no hurry to send either of us to the office for paperwork. Luke and I shared an easy banter, and it was so enjoyable to just chat with him. There was no pressure here, no agenda. It was nice.

Once Jack and the evening staff arrived, I headed to the office to collect my purse and coat. It was unseasonably cold for March. I was really looking forward to spring; my pea coat barely fastened over my growing stomach anymore. Luke met me on my way out of the office.

"Hey, I'm starving. Wanna grab a bite to eat?" he asked.

I felt my pulse begin to quicken. Though Luke had been consistently friendly, even somewhat flirty, at work, we had never hung out beyond the walls of the store. The idea both excited and terrified me.

"Sure," I said, trying to keep the stammer out of my voice.

"Great," he smiled. "There's a place around the block. Do you like Mediterranean?"

"Absolutely," I replied, hoping the baby felt the same way.

Luke and I walked in silence to the restaurant. I tried to talk myself out of the nerves. *This is not a date. He is your boss. Plus, you are the size of a small hippo,* I reminded myself. But I couldn't help recalling the appreciative look in his eyes that morning when he told me I looked great...

The restaurant was small but looked pretty nice, with linen table cloths and tea lights on every table. It possessed an intimate feel and it was pretty busy for so early in the evening. I hoped that was a sign of stellar food. The waiter led us over to a small table near the window, and I was quick to note that Luke held out my chair for me.

I have to say, things like that really do it for me. I know that I'm supposed to be an independent feminist and all of that, but show me a gentleman who practices chivalry and I'm pretty much done for.

"So, Ginny," Luke said, smiling at me over the menu. "How are you enjoying your new job?"

"I love it, Luke," I said eagerly.

"And you're not just saying that 'cause it's my store?" he asked, grinning.

I laughed. "No! Not at all. Seriously, I love working there. I never knew how much fun it would be to talk about books all day."

"I'm glad. It seems like you enjoy it, but I wondered if I was reading you right."

"What about you? What made you decide to buy a bookstore?" I asked, wondering if I would finally find out the reasons behind his apparent antipathy toward his job.

"Oh, I didn't buy it," he said quickly. "It's actually my dad's place."

I didn't bother to try and hide my surprise. I'd been working there for several weeks and I had never heard anything about his father. "Really? So your dad is my boss?"

"I guess," Luke answered, scratching his neck.

"So why haven't I met him?"

Luke sighed. "He had a heart attack six months ago."

I gasped. "Oh, Luke, I'm so sorry. I shouldn't have asked."

He smiled. "Don't worry about it. Of course you asked; you work there. Besides, he's doing fine now."

"Oh good," I said, relieved.

"But the doctor said he had to retire, take it easy. His whole life was that store, it was too much stress." Luke's forehead wrinkled. "So I stepped in and took over the day to day stuff."

Ah. Well, that explains a lot. "Let me guess," I said, hoping I wasn't overstepping my bounds. "This wouldn't have been your first choice if nothing had happened to him."

He smiled at me. "How'd you know?" he said.

"Just a hunch."

Luke laughed. "Have I been that obvious?"

"No, I just get the sense you don't always want to be there."

Our food arrived then, and conversation diminished for a while as we focused on our meals. I had ordered a stuffed meatball called a kibbeh, which I had never had before. It was delicious. I hoped the baby would agree—he had a tendency of keeping me awake all night when he wasn't happy with my food choices.

"So, Ginny," Luke said eventually, once we had slowed our eating a bit. "Can I ask you something personal?"

"Sure," I shrugged, leaning back from my meal and taking a drink of pop.

"This baby...what's the story there?" Luke sounded kind of awkward—and really curious.

I swallowed my pop. "What do you mean?" I asked.

He definitely looked awkward now. "I was just curious. You've never said anything about a guy, and you don't talk about the pregnancy much. I wasn't sure if you were excited, or..." Luke's face was getting red, so I decided I would put him out of his misery.

"The father is my ex-boyfriend. He's not involved with the baby." I tried very hard not to think about those words as I said them. "I'm kind of scared, because I'm doing this on my own. But I'm very excited about the baby."

"You must be pretty brave," he said, shaking his head. "I can't imagine doing something like that alone."

"Well, I guess I'm not really alone," I clarified. "I live with my two best friends, and they help me out a lot." I smiled, thinking about the girls. "Actually, I would say that they're a lot better to have around than a clueless guy."

Luke chuckled softly. "So this ex...is he a total bastard, or what?'

"I never would have thought he was," I said, wishing he hadn't brought it up. "But all evidence now seems to point that way."

Unexpectedly, Luke reached over and grabbed my hand. "I'm sorry, Ginny," he said softly, and his eyes did that flashy thing I loved so much. "But I have to say it. If this guy is willing to give you up, regardless of the circumstances, he's insane."

I felt warmth spread through me, right from Luke's hand into my chest. "Thanks," I said.

He grinned again. "Just stating the obvious."

Chapter Twenty

Twenty-four Weeks: Your baby (and your bump!) continue to grow at a phenomenal rate! At this point, your baby probably weighs more than a pound. Your stomach is getting more and more prominent. As he watches your body change so drastically, your hubby may be wondering how he can be more involved in the pregnancy. Don't be afraid to ask him for help! Have you involved your husband in decisions about how you will decorate Baby's room? There are few ways better to get your hubby involved in the preparations for your little one's arrival!—Dr. Rebecca Carr, A Gal's Guide to a Fabulous First Pregnancy!

"It looks like a stork exploded in here," Annie said disdainfully.

I had to agree with her. We were standing in the entrance to Baby and Me! and it was definitely very overwhelming.

"What did you expect it would look like?" Jen asked. "It's a baby store. Did you think they would have camping gear?"

I laughed as we moved further into the store.

"What exactly are we looking for?" Annie asked, picking up a weird U-shaped pillow. "And what the heck is this for?" We all peered at it in confusion.

"Hello!" said a bubbly voice behind us. We turned as one to face a cheerful woman whose nametag identified her as LeeAnn. "Are you looking for a boppy today?"

"What the hell is a boppy?" Annie asked.

"Fifty cents!" I cried. Annie flipped me off.

LeeAnn looked flustered for a moment, but soon glued her toothpaste ad smile back on. "That pillow is a boppy. They're very popular."

"But what are they for?" Jen asked, puzzled.

"For the baby!" LeeAnn enthused. "You can sit her up in it, or use it to prop her for nursing. They have tons of uses!"

"Well, we're not really in the market for a bop thing today," I said. "We were wondering where your cribs are."

"Oh, you're expecting!" LeeAnn gushed, looking me over for the first time. "How exciting! How far along are you? Eight months?"

I glared at her as Annie stifled a laugh. "I'm twenty four weeks." LeeAnn had the good grace to look uncomfortable.

She led us quickly to the crib section and then disappeared to help someone else, probably afraid of me and my inappropriate, boppy-incompetent friends.

The crib section was overwhelming. They had every make and model imaginable. Cribs that turned into beds, cribs that cost 2,000 bucks, white cribs, wood cribs. "Jesus," I muttered. "I have no idea what I'm looking for."

Jen, ever prepared, pulled out a computer print-out from her purse. "I found these recommendations online," she explained, passing me the paper. "It says the best crib for safety doesn't have to be very expensive. We just need to look out for those factors."

I looked at the sheet she had given me. It was full of information about slat distance, drop sides, safety seals. "Jen," I said, passing it back. "I have no idea what any of this means."

She rolled her eyes at me but took the paper back. "Why don't you find one you like, that fits your budget, and we can go from there."

We walked around the crib section. Annie tried to convince me to buy a Vera Wang designed crib, but it was definitely not in the budget. The budget, in fact, was pretty pathetic. I had been saving a bit of money from all of my paychecks, but it wasn't much. I planned to get as much baby gear as possible from garage sales and resale shops, but Jen had insisted some things needed to be new—apparently safety was an important aspect in items like cribs and car seats. Who knew?

Finally my eyes came to rest on a simple, maple wood crib. They had it set up with the most gorgeous bedding—shades of blue and brown, patterned in polka dots and stripes. No cartoon animals, no sports themes or airplanes. It looked sophisticated and darling at the same time. The bedding was perfect. It was also obscenely expensive. The crib, though, was reasonably priced.

I called Jen over, and she consulted her research. "It looks pretty good to me," she said finally. "But we should probably ask someone..." She set off to find LeeAnn, who quickly confirmed that the crib was, in fact, very safe. Better still, it was on sale. We bought it immediately.

I couldn't get that expensive bedding out of my head as we waited in the checkout line. It was exactly what I would have chosen if I had an unlimited budget. The blue matched my own comforter perfectly, which was important because the baby was going to be living in my room—our rental house was only three bedrooms, so we didn't exactly have space for a nursery. I was fine with it, to be honest. I was already starting to have anxiety dreams about the myriad of disasters that could befall my baby. I was sure I'd be able to relax more the closer he was to me.

Annie and Jen heaved the crib box out to Jen's jeep. With the backseat down, they managed to wedge it in. Unfortunately, this left Annie without a seat. She crammed herself on the floor between the box and the back of my chair. "This is just like us," she huffed, trying to get comfortable without being squashed by the heavy box. "We just always have to do everything the classy way."

Back at home, the girls once again struggled with the box, panting as they heaved it up the front steps and into the house. I stood by and made helpful suggestions, mostly about how stupid they looked.

When they finally got it into the house, they both collapsed on the couch and demanded lemonade. I brought us each a glass and we sat together, staring at the giant box, which now took up half the living room.

"Um," Annie started. "Do either of you actually have any idea how to put this thing together?"

Jen and I were silent for a moment. "I'm sure we can figure it out," she said finally. "We're three college-educated, smart women."

"Who don't own any tools," Annie muttered under her breath.

We sat down in front of the box, pulling out various pieces and trying to match them to the pictures in the directions. We determined that we would, in fact, need tools, so Annie ran next door to see what she could borrow from our neighbors.

It took us four hours. Four hours and a bottle and a half of wine. Not for me, unfortunately, but Annie and Jen had started drinking shortly after we failed, for the third time, to properly attach bracket C to leg brace F.

"Why do they have to make this so hard?" Jen demanded. "It's ridiculous! If three college-educated, smart, successful women can't figure it out, who can?" The more she drank, the more adjectives she added to her description of us. Annie, on the other hand, became more and more cheerful as her wine flowed. Neither was very helpful.

Somehow we managed to get it together. I could only hope we did it right. "Crib falling apart around baby" was a new anxiety dream I was sure I would be adding to my repertoire that night.

"We did it!" Jen enthused proudly, putting her arm around me.

"Yeah," Annie agreed, hiccupping. "And we don't even have any pieces left over!"

Chapter Twenty-one

After that first dinner with Luke, my anxiety about hanging out with him outside of work faded pretty fast. It would have to, as I was now seeing him after work just about every day. He would even show up to meet me after my shift when he wasn't on the schedule.

Some nights we would go and get coffee together, sitting and talking about books and films for hours. Other times we went for dinner or to catch an early movie. So far, all of our outings were still tied to work—he had never called me at home or asked to see me on a night I wasn't already at the shop. But slowly, very slowly, I could feel us getting closer.

He was so easy to talk to, and we had a ton in common. We both loved books, craft beers, and international food. We had the same taste in movies— and as an avid movie-lover, this was very important to me. I could never do with a man who liked blow-up action crap. Our upbringings were vastly different, but we both had the distinct honor of being disappointments to our parents.

"What I had really wanted to do was to go to culinary school," Luke admitted one evening over cheesecake. We had both worked a double shift, staying at the store long past closing as we tried to complete the inventory. Luke had ordered in dinner for us from the diner down the street, and we ate sitting cross-legged on the floor in the middle of the shelves.

"Really?" I asked.

"Don't sound so shocked," he laughed. "I'm a really good cook!"

"Then why didn't you go?" I asked.

Luke sighed. "My parents didn't approve," he said. "My dad wanted me to take over the store someday. He said if he was paying for my education, I was going to major in business."

"That sucks," I said. "Didn't he think being a chef was a worthwhile option?"

He laughed, sounding bitter. "No, not at all. He told me cooking was fine for a hobby, but not something to make a living out of."

"I'm sorry, Luke," I said, knowing full well how horrible it was when your parents brushed aside your feelings.

He shrugged. "It wasn't too bad. I liked school, even though I thought the business classes were boring as hell." He smiled at me. "But I got a good job when I graduated—well, not an enjoyable one, but one that made me some pretty good money."

"That's always a good thing," I replied, thinking it was out of character for him to care much about money when it came to describing a job as "good."

"It *was* a good thing," he replied. "Because I got to save a ton. I had the perfect plan: I was going to save as much as possible until I could afford to go on a tour of Europe. If my dad wasn't willing to pay for me to learn cooking, I was going to get out and learn it myself, in the real world."

"That sounds amazing," I breathed. "God, I've always wanted to travel, especially to Europe. I've never been anywhere."

"Me either," he said, and the bitterness was very pronounced in his voice now. "I was a few months from having enough cash when my dad had his heart attack."

"Oh, God," I muttered. "Oh, Luke, that's horrible. I'm so sorry."

He didn't meet my eyes. "So instead I ended up here, running my dad's store in the same town I grew up in, spending half my day trying to deal with numbers and invoices..." He exhaled deeply, clenching his fist.

I felt so bad for him. He was stuck here out of duty, and it was the last place in the world he wanted to be. Instinctively, I reached out and grabbed his hand.

Luke looked up at me in surprise, then smiled. "Well, it could be worse," he said. "It's good to have a job, right?"

I nodded.

"And at least my dad owned a business I could stand. I love books. What if he had owned a plumbing store or something?"

I laughed. "Yeah, that would have been worse."

"Besides," he said, his voice growing slightly husky as he squeezed my hand gently. "It's been a lot more bearable at the store lately."

I felt my heart start to beat more quickly, and I couldn't help but grin at him.

"So," I said, trying to bring the conversation back to safer ground, "what kind of stuff do you like to cook?"

"My specialty is Asian fusion," he said, his voice quickly becoming intense. "But I like to make all different kinds of food. So long as it's real food, not pretentious, flouncy stuff."

I laughed. "That sounds like my kind of meal,"

"Maybe I could cook for you sometime," he said, somewhat shyly, looking down at his lap. I felt a familiar warmth in my cheeks.

"I would really like that," I said softly. He looked up and our eyes met. He held my gaze for a beat longer than was completely comfortable, and I felt the heat in my cheeks increase.

"Good," he said, smiling at me. "How about this weekend?"

I gulped. I wasn't scheduled at the store this weekend. If I was going to see him, it would be completely independent of work. I swallowed again, wondering if that was a step I wanted to take. Who was I kidding? Of course I *wanted* to take it, but I wondered if it was smart to do so. I tried to picture what Jen would say, but Luke was still looking at me, waiting for an answer, his eyes intense and fixed on my face. It was very hard to be rational, or even form coherent thought, when he was looking at me like that.

"Sounds perfect," I murmured.

* * *

We arranged to meet at Luke's apartment that Saturday at seven. I felt nervous all day, my stomach a fluttery mess. The baby joined in on the party, moving around like crazy and adding to my discomfort.

I took special care getting ready. I didn't have many outfits that could minimize my bump anymore, but I did have a few things that emphasized my cleavage. After much trying on and hemming and hawing, I decided to go for it. I tried to keep my make-up minimal, but I couldn't help getting into the mood: it had been so long since I had dressed up for a guy. I wanted to feel, and look, pretty.

It was all worth it when I saw Luke's face. He very obviously appreciated the effort I had put in to my appearance. It was a look that I had once known well, the look of a guy who was thinking that I looked great. Before Josh (who I was *not* going to think about that night), it was a look I saw all the time. Hell, Josh himself looked at me like that practically every day— but no, I wasn't thinking about that. I was with Luke tonight, and that was where my attention was going to stay.

Luke's apartment was great. It took up most of the second floor of a brownstone in the downtown area of Rochester, very close to the store. His furniture was very eclectic, and I figured it was a mix of hand-me-downs and cheap stuff, probably Ikea. Unsurprisingly, the walls were crowded with bookshelves. He had hung several framed maps of different European countries around the room. I liked it immediately—it was the type of apartment that just felt like its owner.

He ushered me into the kitchen and sat me down at the small table with a glass of water. "Luke," I said, practically moaning. "It smells amazing in here!"

"And you had the gall to doubt me!" he chided.

"I'm sorry. Clearly, I was way mistaken."

"Well, you haven't tasted it yet," he said. "Maybe you'll actually think I suck."

I laughed. "I doubt that. Nothing that sucks could smell this good. What are you making, anyhow?"

"Paella," he said proudly. "I've been slaving away half the day."

"Oh my God." I did moan this time. "I love paella!"

"Good!" Luke turned back to the stove, removing a lid from the pan there and stirring. "It should be almost done. I didn't use seafood, just sausage and chicken. I wasn't sure if seafood was good for you, or for the baby."

I was touched. My doctor had told me most seafood was fine in moderation, but it was still a nice gesture.

"You know what I think is kind of amazing?" I asked impulsively. "You never seem weirded out by this."

"Weirded out by what?"

"The whole pregnancy thing," I said. "You don't ignore it, but it's like it doesn't faze you or something."

Luke shrugged. "I guess that's because it doesn't," he replied. "Faze me, that is. Maybe it would have been different if I'd known you before, but I didn't. You've been pregnant since we met so I guess it just seems like part of you."

I laughed. "I wish it felt that normal to me."

Luke put the top back on the pan and came and sat down across from me. "Does it still seem strange to you?" he asked.

I shrugged. "Sometimes. This is definitely not what I thought I would be doing, you know?"

"Sometimes those unexpected things are the best part," he said. "I mean, if you would have asked either of us a year ago, I bet neither one of us would have imagined we'd be working at the store. And then we never would have met. We wouldn't be here together now."

At his words, I had a sudden vision of myself a year ago. A year ago, I was with Josh, and very much in love. I felt a pang at the thought, a deep pain in my chest. I tried to push it away.

Luke reached out and took my hand, staring intently into my eyes. "I'm glad I'm here with you," he said softly.

I tried to smile. "Me too," I said. And I meant it. Mostly.

*　*　*

It was a wonderful meal. I managed to get Josh out of my head eventually, and I was so glad I did because Luke was great. He made me laugh and he made me feel beautiful. And the food was delicious.

137

At the end of the evening, he walked me to the door and pulled me in for a hug. "I had a really good time," he murmured into my hair.

"Me too," I said, as he pulled back. "Thank you so much for dinner."

"You're welcome," he said, tucking a piece of hair behind my ear. I shivered at his touch. He really was a gorgeous man. "Can I see you tomorrow?"

"Sure," I breathed. He was standing very close to me, and the largeness of him, the maleness of him, overwhelmed me. He smelled good—a mixture of the Spanish spices he had cooked with and some kind of musky body wash. His hand, which lingered on my face, felt strong.

Then he was leaning down, his face coming closer, and closer. I wanted to feel his lips on mine, I craved it with my entire body. But at the last minute, I turned my head, causing his lips to brush my cheek instead. I'm not sure why.

He pulled back, looking slightly surprised. But then he smiled at me. "Drive safe," he said. "I'll pick you up tomorrow at one, okay?"

"Perfect," I said, smiling at him briefly before turning to go.

Chapter Twenty-two

Just as promised, Luke was at the house the next day at one. Annie and Jen had camped out at the window to catch sight of him when he pulled up.

"The two of you are ridiculous," I informed them as I scurried around, gathering my things.

"It's your own fault," Annie said. "You told us this was the hottest guy you've ever seen. Did you honestly think we weren't going to want to check him out?"

I couldn't deny she had a point. "Where the hell are my shoes?" I moaned, rifling through the front closet. "This is silly, I just had them..."

"Ooh, I think he's here!" Jen squealed.

"Shit!" I said, standing up quickly. "I'm not ready!"

"I guess he'll just have to come in," Annie said smugly. "And you owe me a dollar."

I groaned. "Alright, listen, you two," I said firmly as I heard Luke's car door slam outside. "If you do anything to embarrass me, I will kill you. Seriously."

Annie snorted but was prevented from replying by a knock on the door.

"We'll be good, I promise," Jen said, smiling at me as she went to let Luke in.

She opened the front door and I heard her draw in her breath sharply. "Hi," she said breathily. "I'm Jen, Ginny's roommate. Come on in."

"Hi, Jen, I'm Luke," he responded from the porch. She stepped aside and Luke entered the room.

I couldn't blame Jen for being flustered. Luke looked great today, even better than normal. He was wearing jeans and a blue sweater over a white dress shirt. The white of the shirt stood out markedly against his tan skin, and the sweater made his eyes look particularly blue. It wasn't just that Luke was attractive, it was his entire demeanor. I don't know how to describe it except to say that he was very, very male. He towered over the three of us, and I could practically feel the girls go all fluttery next to me.

"Hey, Luke," I said, trying to keep my voice light.

He beamed at me. "Hi, Ginny. You look great."

I blushed and looked down. For God's sake, why did I have to constantly act like a twelve-year-old girl around him?

Across the room, I heard Annie clear her throat infinitesimally. "Oh, Luke, this is Annie, my other roommate."

"Hi," she practically purred, sliding up next to him. "I've heard a lot about you." I glared at her, but Luke just smiled.

"I've heard a lot about you guys, too," he said pleasantly.

"So where are you two off to?" she asked, moving slightly closer to him. God, she could be irritating.

"I thought we'd go to the zoo today," Luke addressed me, raising his eyebrows as if to ask me what I thought.

"I haven't been to the zoo in forever!" I said, excited. The Detroit Zoo was located in Royal Oak, right down the road from us, but I hadn't gone since I was a kid.

"It's supposed to actually feel a little like spring today," he said. "I thought it would be nice to be outside."

"That sounds perfect," I said. "Let me just grab a jacket." I hurried up to my room, praying that Annie wouldn't do anything too embarrassing in my absence. I found the pair of shoes I had been looking for, laid out neatly at the end of my bed, exactly where I had put them in anticipation of getting ready. Figures. Glancing one last time in the mirror, I fluffed my hair and headed out of the room to meet my date.

* * *

Luke had gotten it right: the weather was beautiful, our first nice day of the season. The zoo wasn't very crowded but there was a pleasant vibe in the air.

"I love Michigan in the spring," Luke said, taking my hand as we walked through the main concourse area. "The minute we get some fifty degree weather everyone stumbles outside like they've never seen the sun before."

Luke had a point. It was a tradition around here. The sun would finally show itself, however so dimly, and suddenly you'd see people in shorts wherever you looked, and the windows of every car you passed would be rolled down.

Since I hadn't been to the zoo in so long, I wanted to see everything. I remembered that when I was a kid, the chimps were my favorite, so we started there. As we walked from exhibit to exhibit, Luke held my hand and we chatted about animals we had known. I discovered that Luke's family had always kept dogs, and he wished he could get one of his own. My parents had never allowed me to have a pet and I told him how jealous I used to get of Annie and her family's two cats when we were little.

We rode on the train, ate ice cream, and spent a good half-hour sitting comfortably in the butterfly house as the colorful wings flapped around us, making us laugh when they landed on our arms and hands. It was one of the nicest afternoons I'd had in a long time.

As he had been there more recently, Luke led the way around the animal exhibits. "They're all really active today," he told me as we stood in front of the tiger den. "It's actually better to come to the zoo when it's still kind of cold out because most of the animals move around more. In the summer, they get lazy and they're harder to see."

Once we'd had our fill of the tigers, apes, reptiles and giraffes, Luke took my hand again. "You have to see the Arctic Ring of Life," he told me. "It's my favorite. I think you'll really like it." He led me along a winding outdoor path through the exhibit. After a few moments without a sign of life around us, I started to feel slightly disappointed. "Just wait," Luke promised.

We entered a dark building and followed a group of school-aged kids into an underground gallery. There were windows spaced along the walls, allowing us to see out into the enclosure we had just walked through. Luke led me deeper into the room until we reached what appeared to be a brightly lit hallway.

As we stepped through the doorway, I gasped: it wasn't a hallway at all, it was a glass tunnel. We were surrounded by water and swimming right over our head was a huge, white polar bear. I couldn't help but let out a little squeal. "Oh, Luke," I cried. "Look!"

I was completely enthralled. I led him as close to the glass walls as we could get and stared in awe as the bear continued to swim around us. "This is amazing!" I breathed. "I've lived here all my life, how have I never known this existed?"

"Ginny," Luke whispered. There was something in his voice, something heavy and tense. I looked up at him in surprise to see him staring intently at my face. I wondered how long he had been watching me like that. "I think *you're* amazing."

Luke was going to kiss me. I knew it. And I wanted him to.

He leaned down and I tilted my face toward him, closing my eyes just as his mouth touched mine. His lips were soft against my own, but I could feel heat there, just below the surface, as he pressed closer to me.

He was a wonderful kisser, perfect really. So I couldn't figure out why it was Josh's face that flashed, with perfect clarity, before my closed eyelids, in the moment that Luke kissed me.

Chapter Twenty-three

Twenty-eight Weeks: Get ready for the third trimester! In the coming weeks you'll start to notice some big changes as you move ever closer to that due date! You may begin to experience itchy skin, swollen feet, leg cramps, and heartburn. Not fun! But I promise none of this will matter to you once you're holding that precious baby! Dads—this is a hard time of the pregnancy for Mom—make sure you help her as much as you can. Foot massages and belly rubs will improve her outlook considerably!—Dr. Rebecca Carr, *A Gal's Guide to a Fabulous First Pregnancy!*

"How ya doing?" Luke asked, looking over at me in the passenger seat.

"Not too bad," I muttered, rubbing at my chest.

"I guess barbeque was a bad idea, huh?" he said sheepishly.

"Yeah, I guess so," I laughed.

Luke reached across the gear shift to hold my hand. "Sorry, Ginny," he said, brushing my palm with his thumb. "That was stupid of me. I should have picked somewhere else."

It was a rainy Saturday afternoon in early May. Luke had taken me down to the city to try his favorite restaurant, Slows, an amazing barbeque place. The food had been wonderful, and I'm afraid I made a bit of a pig out of myself. After we ate, we spent the afternoon wandering around the Detroit Institute of Arts. It was lovely, the perfect date.

Until my feet had decided to swell up to double their size and a wicked case of heartburn had overtaken me.

"It's not your fault, Luke," I said, squeezing his hand. "I'm the one that should have known better." I sighed. "Honestly, I'm not very good at this whole thing. I bet most moms-to-be would know that eating a huge lunch with tons of sodium and spices is not a good idea, especially when you follow it up with a few hours of walking."

Luke glanced down at my feet. "Maybe it's time to stop with the heels," he added.

I glared at him. "This pregnancy may take away my figure and my ability to eat what I like, but it will not take away my shoes."

He grinned at me quickly, before turning his eyes back to the road. "Well, we'll be home soon and you can put your feet up and take some antacids."

It should not have felt weird to me that Luke referred to my place as home. I knew he didn't mean it literally, and besides, in the last two weeks Luke had gotten very comfortable in our little yellow house.

We spent most of our evenings there now, whether we had worked together or not. It was pretty much understood that Luke would meet me there as soon as we were both free. Sometimes we went out, exploring restaurants and cafes. Luke took me to a few low-key concerts, but the heat in the clubs bothered me, so oftentimes we would just stay in so Luke could cook for me. Later, we would snuggle on the couch and watch TV or head out to the movies. It felt comfortable, natural.

The girls loved having him around. Annie continued to flirt unabashedly, and Jen had recently managed to say several words to him without blushing or stammering.

Luke seemed completely enamored with me. He doted on me all the time. Whenever we were together he was doing things for me: cooking meals, bringing me drinks and snacks whenever we were watching movies. He was constantly touching me, his hand absently brushing against my arms, my hair, my hands. On the rare occasions we were apart, he would call or text just to chat or check in with me.

We had only been together for a few weeks, but he was the perfect boyfriend. And I should have been thrilled.

We arrived at the house and Luke, ever the gentleman, insisted on opening my door and helping me out and up the front steps. Once we got inside he deposited me on the couch—the man literally put a pillow under my feet, can you believe it? He then proceeded to hunt down some antacids and make me a huge glass of chocolate milk (he thought he read somewhere that milk helped heartburn).

Once I was all settled, Luke joined me on the couch and transferred my feet from the pillow over to his lap. Rubbing them gently, he smiled at me. "There. How's that?" I smiled back, though I felt a little overwhelmed by his perfection.

"Great. Thanks, Luke."

As he rubbed my tired feet, I looked down at my body. I felt huge today. My stomach continued to take over my entire figure and I was noticing my face and arms were swelling out as well. And my ass was just out of control.

"Why do you put up with this?" I wondered out loud.

"With what?" Luke asked.

I gestured at myself. "With this," I said. "You're a gorgeous guy, Luke. Why on earth are you spending your time with someone like me?

Luke looked puzzled. "I don't get it," he said.

"Luke, in my experience guys who look like you prefer to spend their time with girls who are pretty. I don't know of any other guy who would want to be with a girl as gigantic and disgusting as me."

He rolled his eyes. "First of all, I don't want to hang out with 'girls who are pretty,' " he said. "Not when I can hang out with a girl that is beautiful."

It was my turn to roll my eyes.

"I'm serious!" he exclaimed, offended. "You have to know that you're beautiful."

"Luke," I said distinctly. "I'm *pregnant.*"

"No, really?" he gasped. "I never would have noticed!"

I tried to slap his arm, but he merely grabbed my hand and held it tight.

"Listen to me, Ginny, okay? I know you don't feel like yourself. But you are beautiful. You have been since the day I met you. And just because your belly has gotten bigger since then, it doesn't make you less gorgeous to me. Okay?"

I stared at him. How could anyone be this perfect? He leaned in closer to me and whispered in my ear. "I know we have to take things slow, because of the baby. I'm fine with that, Ginny." His voice was low and intense in my ear, making my tummy feel funny. "You're not going to be pregnant forever. And when this is over, I'll still be there. I promise."

He moved to lean back again, but I caught his face in my hands and kissed him. I wanted to show him how amazing I thought he was, how thankful I felt that he was here with me. He must have picked up on some of that, because he smiled warmly at me when he pulled away.

"We on the same page now?" he asked.

I nodded.

"Good. Let's find something to watch while you rest."

Luke flipped through the channels until he found a travel documentary on Eastern Europe. "This look good?" he asked.

"Whatever," I murmured, closing my eyes. "I'm actually pretty tired. Would you mind...?"

"Not at all," he said, leaning over and kissing my forehead. "You just rest. I'll be right here."

I dreamt of Josh.

We were up in the northern part of the state at the Straits of Mackinac, the stretch of water connecting Lake Michigan and Lake Huron. We had gone there for vacation one summer, staying at a cheap hotel on the water. We ate at hole-in-the-wall restaurants every night, walked around the little town of Mackinac and swam in the freezing water each day.

In my dream, we were having a picnic. We were stretched out on the grass at the state park, right along the shore. In the distance we could see the Mackinac Bridge, connecting the two peninsulas. The sun felt warm on my skin and Josh was brushing my hair away from my face.

"You're beautiful," he whispered, and even after all this time, the memory of his voice was crystal clear in my head.

This was the feeling I could never properly explain to my girlfriends, to the people who wondered why someone like me would want to settle down so early. Josh loved me. He honestly and truly loved me. It was like he could see inside of me, he could see the bits of my heart that no one else had ever noticed, not even the girls.

Being around someone like that was intoxicating, and that's how I felt in my dream. Delirious with the knowledge that someone as smart and honest as Josh could love me in the way that he did. I felt like a better person than I really was, like all of the crap I had done in my past just didn't matter anymore.

With Josh, everything was simple. He loved me, I loved him. We enjoyed every moment that we spent together. We showed each other new things, taught each other, made every day about laughter and kindness to each other. It was beautiful, what we had together, and I could feel that beauty so clearly in my dream.

"I love you, Josh," I whispered—but Josh was gone. The dream was shifting, the scene changing. I was no longer sitting with Josh, basking in the sun and in his love. Instead I was sitting next to the water, watching the waves crash around the boats out in the straits. The sun had gone down and I was completely alone.

I woke up with such an intense pain in my heart that it took my breath away.

"You okay?" Luke asked, leaning toward me.

"Yeah," I gasped. "Bad dream, I guess."

He resumed his rubbing of my feet. "You're okay, sweetie. Everything's fine."

I told myself he was right. Of course everything was fine. I had wonderful friends, a great job, a baby on the way, and a beautiful man sitting next to me, a man who gave every indication that he was crazy about me. There was no reason, absolutely no reason at all, that I should feel such a pang of longing for the one thing that I had lost.

Chapter Twenty-four

It was true what those damn baby books said: I was feeling much worse these days. I had officially entered my third trimester and it brought with it swollen feet, an overactive bladder, achy joints, and an alarmingly large stomach.

Work was starting to become more of a strain. I felt like I had to pee every five minutes and it was getting harder and harder to pull myself up from whatever chair I had plopped in to talk to customers or make a sale. I noticed Luke was spending more time in the store than was completely necessary. I had a feeling he was trying to help me out as much as possible, and I appreciated it immensely.

I returned home one Wednesday, exhausted and looking forward to nothing more than a warm bath and an early date with my bed. Jen was sitting in the living room when I opened the front door, and her expression told me the bath was going to have to wait.

"Catherine called," she said without preamble.

I groaned. I hadn't spoken with my mother since I had broken the news about the baby and subsequently hung up on her. "What did she want?" I asked.

"She asked about you, wanted to know how you were."

"How nice of her," I sneered.

"She wanted you to call her. I told her I would tell you."

The last thing in the world I wanted to do was talk to my mother, but I figured I may as well get it over with so I could enjoy my night. I took my cell phone up to my room and sat on the bed, sighing dramatically before dialing her number.

"Hello, Mother," I said when she had answered. "Jen told me that you called."

"Virginia." She sounded surprised to hear from me, as if she had expected I would ignore her. "I'm glad you called."

There was an uncomfortable silence. I so badly wanted her to apologize for the horrible thing she had said to me. Since I had fallen so completely in love with my son, her insult had only rankled me more. However, I knew from long experience that if I waited for her to say sorry first, I would be waiting for a very, very long time.

"Mom, I'm sorry I hung up on you," I said in resignation. "And I'm sorry I told you the news the way I did."

She cleared her throat several times. "I'm sorry, too," she finally replied. "I was just shocked, that's all."

"I know. I should have handled it better."

I couldn't say it was a breakthrough conversation, but at least it didn't end with us screaming at each other. She asked how I was feeling, if I had the things I needed for the baby. I explained that I was saving up a bit at a time but that I had a lot of the basics—which wasn't strictly true. Outside of the crib, I was pretty much screwed.

We hung up on polite, if not amicable, terms. I headed down to tell Jen how things had gone.

She was sitting on the couch with a pile of blue and brown in her hands, her head bent over the fabric as she worked. "What are you doing?" I asked, and she jumped in surprise.

"Shit!" she exclaimed. "I thought you'd be longer. You weren't supposed to see this!"

"What is it?" I walked over to the couch to get a closer look. The fabric was patterned in blue and brown stripes and it looked vaguely familiar.

She sighed. "It's a baby blanket."

I could only stare at her.

"Look, I know it's not as good as what we saw in the store that day." She looked uncomfortable. "But I went to the fabric store and I saw this, and it looked pretty similar. I knew you would never just let me buy the bedding for you, but I thought if I made it you might—"

Before she could say another word, I grabbed her, pulling her into a tight hug. "I can't believe you're doing this," I said softly against her shoulder as my eyes filled with tears. "This is, like, the nicest thing ever."

Jen squeezed me back, briefly, before pulling away and averting her eyes. "It's not that big a deal," she said, but her voice shook and gave her away.

"It is a big deal, Jen," I replied, wiping my eyes. "Thank you."

"You're welcome," she said, smiling slightly as she busied herself with the blanket once more. I curled up against her on the couch, all thoughts of my bath gone. She was playing soft music while she worked, and it was so comfortable and nice to be sitting there with her. I'd been spending so much time with Luke, I felt like I wasn't seeing her enough lately.

"So, how's the hot man?" she asked, as if reading my thoughts.

"He's good," I replied. "He's working the late shift tonight."

"Is he coming over after?" she asked. I shrugged, but we both knew he probably would. He always did.

"How are things going with the two of you?" she asked, and I thought I caught a bit of a tone in her voice.

"It's going good," I answered carefully. "He's really nice to me."

She didn't say anything for a moment. "It's pretty clear he's crazy about you," she finally said. I shrugged again. "How do you feel about him?"

I looked at her closely. She continued to sew, as if she had no idea I was watching her, but I had a feeling she understood a lot more than she was letting on.

"I'm not sure," I sighed. "I mean, on paper, this is perfect. He really likes me, he treats me great, we have a lot in common..."

"He's totally gorgeous," she added.

"Yeah, that. But...I don't know. I don't know how I feel."

"That was kind of the feeling I got," she said.

It was true, what I told her—on paper, Luke was perfect. And I was having a lot of fun with him. I couldn't deny his attention was flattering...But sometimes, it all felt like too much. Could a person be *too* perfect?

It was great that Luke wanted to spend so much time with me, but every once in a while, it grated on me. Like when he always wanted to pick the places we would go to. Or the few times when I said I wanted a quiet night in and he invited himself over anyhow. But I'm sure I'm just being silly.

"That's okay, you know that, right?" Jen continued, drawing me from my thoughts.

"What?"

"To be unsure. To not fall head over heels just because some gorgeous guy likes you."

"It feels like I'm being really spoiled," I muttered. "I mean, what else could I ask for?" Jen raised her eyebrows at me. "Come on," I said. "What are the chances that *any* guy would be interested me in my current state, let alone someone so perfect? Don't you think turning him down would be pretty ridiculous?"

"Ginny," she said slowly. "You've been through a lot this year, you know? Your life is totally in upheaval. I'm glad you can have fun with Luke and he treats you so nice. But honestly, I'd be a lot more worried about you if you did tell me you were crazy about him."

"Really?" I asked. "Why?"

"Because I would assume you were trying to bury your problems in a guy," she said quietly, looking up from the blanket at last to meet my eyes. I felt my breath catch. I knew what she was talking about—it's what I always used to do, before Josh. When I was upset about my parents, or feeling lonely, or unhappy with my life, I would find some random, gorgeous guy to hide in for a while.

"You've changed, Ginny," she said firmly. "You have. Can you see that?" When I didn't respond, she smiled at me. "I can see it, even if you can't. You're a different person, you really are."

I couldn't think what to say to that. Was she right, or just trying to make me feel better?

"Anyhow," she said, turning back to the blanket. "I think you should just chill out here tonight and keep me company."

And that's exactly what I did.

Chapter Twenty-five

Thirty Weeks: You're getting so close now! If you're like the majority of mommies, your excitement is probably starting to compete with nerves as you consider the approaching birth! It's a great idea to sit down with Daddy and come up with a birthing plan. How do you envision your baby's birth? Will you use drugs or will you try it au natural? *Would you like to try a water birth? Who will be in the delivery room with you? You probably also want to think about packing a hospital bag. Ladies, you don't want to get stuck at the hospital without your cutest PJs or your must-have moisturizer!*—Dr. Rebecca Carr, *A Gal's Guide to a Fabulous First Pregnancy!*

"I don't think I can watch this!" I told Annie seriously.

"If you can't watch it, how are you going to be able to do it?" she asked.

"Who said I'm going to be able to do it?" I shot back.

"Of course you'll be able to do it," Jen scoffed. "Now shut up, and let's at least try this."

She sat on the couch between Annie and me and pointed the remote at the DVD player. "You ready?"

she asked, sounding slightly nervous herself. I nodded mutely and she pressed play.

For the next ten minutes we sat in silent horror as we watched the most disgusting, disturbing, terrible scene I have ever seen in my life. I thought for sure I was going to throw up, but I was glued to the couch, frozen with shock. At last, Jen seemed unable to take anymore: she pressed the power button and our TV reverted to black screened safety.

"Are you kidding me?" I whispered. "That wasn't real, was it?" I looked at my two best friends. Both of them looked every bit as terrified as I was.

"I think I'm going to be sick," Annie muttered, putting her head in her hands. "I mean, that's like, *seriously* fucked up."

I was too horrified to mention that she owed me a dollar.

"They had to be exaggerating," Jen finally said. "I mean, if childbirth is really like that, who on earth would ever willingly have a baby? The population would have died out ages ago."

I could only pray she was right. Because there was absolutely no way in hell I was going to go through with...with *that*.

"Okay, so let's be done with that," Jen said, hurriedly putting the DVD back in its case. "What else did your doctor give you?'

I spread out the various forms and pamphlets on the coffee table. My doctor was encouraging me to come up with a birth plan. I thought that whole thing sounded kind of hokey, but when I told the girls about it, they insisted we try.

"Do people actually do this?" Annie asked in wonderment, staring at a pamphlet on water births.

"I guess so," I said, shrugging.

"Are you interested in that?" Jen asked, looking over at the pamphlet skeptically.

"No," I said, shaking my head. "No, no. I don't want to go all earth mother here. I want sterile, efficient, standard hospital stuff. I don't want to watch the baby come out, I don't want to practice my breathing. I just want to get this crap over with."

Jen started marking boxes on the form the doctor had given me. "What about your birth partner?" she asked.

"What the hell is a birth partner?" Annie asked.

"Fifty cents!" I pointed at her, causing her to stick out her tongue at me.

"The person who helps you in the delivery room," Jen explained. "Like, who do you want in there with you for the actual labor?"

I looked at both of my friends. "Well, I guess I just assumed...I mean...would you guys go in with me?"

"I had assumed that was the plan," Annie said.

"Don't be silly, of course we will," Jen agreed.

I felt better.

"Okay then," she continued. "I guess the only other thing you need to decide about is the drugs."

I groaned. This was one issue of the birth that I had actually considered. I had been reading in the baby books that drugs were perfectly safe and wouldn't affect the baby. But I couldn't help but feel nervous about it. For the last six months, I hadn't so much as sniffed a cup of coffee in my efforts to keep the baby safe. At my doctor's request, I had avoided sushi, deli meat, even cold medicine. Now, at the very end, was I really going to pump myself full of painkillers?

"I think I'm going to try it without drugs."

"You're insane," Annie said.

"Annie, don't say that!" Jen scolded.

"Look, I'll probably change my mind ten minutes in, but I'm going to at least give it a try," I replied.

"I think that's a very good idea," Jen said, as my cell phone started to ring.

Annie rolled her eyes as I looked at the screen, "Tell Luke I say hi."

I rolled my eyes right back and walked into the hallway as I flipped the phone open. "Hey," I said.

"Hi, Ginny," Luke replied, his voice warm, as it always seemed to be. "How's it going?"

"Pretty good, just hanging out with the girls. How are you?"

"I'm good, almost downtown." Luke and a few of his friends had managed to get tickets to a playoff hockey game that night. "Listen, I wanted to give you a heads-up about something."

"Shoot," I replied.

"My dad is gonna be at the store tomorrow."

"Oh." My heart started racing. I knew that his dad, technically, was my boss, and was completely unrelated to my relationship with Luke, but I still didn't like the sound of this. It seemed too much like meeting the parents.

"He needs to check on the books and the inventory and all that."

"Oh," I said again.

"He's going to love you, Ginny," Luke said softly. "You have absolutely nothing to worry about."

"No, I know," I replied, as my heart continued to pound. "It's no big deal."

"Good. Listen, I gotta run, but I'll call you tonight when I get home, okay?"

"Okay. Have fun tonight."

"Will do. Bye, babe." He hung up, leaving me nearly as unsettled as I had been watching the childbirth video.

No, on second thought, that's ridiculous. Nothing could be as unsettling as the childbirth video.

*   *   *

I arrived at the store early the next morning. Lack of sleep the night before had done little to calm my nerves. Nor had Luke's early phone call. As it turned out, he had had too much fun the night before and was now suffering from a massive hangover. He had assured me he would still make it in, but I was sure he would be late, leaving me alone with his father for God knows how long.

I saw Luke's dad the second I entered the store. Since my conversation with Luke about his dad's cruel insistence that he give up culinary school, I had formed quite a picture in my mind of the elder Mr. Wright. I assumed he would be tall like Luke, but without the warmth or spark that made his son special. I could not have been more wrong.

Luke's dad was standing behind the counter, whistling cheerfully to himself as he ran the till's report. He looked up when the door opened and immediately grinned broadly at me. "You must be Ginny!"

He was a shorter man, maybe around 5'8", with a shock of white hair and a rather generous-looking paunch. His face looked ruddy and covered with the kind of lines that only come from a lifetime of laughing. He wouldn't have looked out of place in a children's storybook.

Mr. Wright dropped the report and hurried around the counter to shake my hand.

"It's so nice to meet you, Luke's told me all about you!" He was practically gushing, and I couldn't help smiling in return, though I felt confused. This was the man that had callously crushed all of Luke's dreams?

"Come and sit down," he urged. "You look exhausted."

I followed him behind the counter and lowered myself into the chair. "Luke tells us you're due in the summer. You must be so excited!"

"Terrified is more like it," I laughed, and he joined me.

"Can't say I blame you," he said. "I'm not ashamed to admit I was always very relieved it was my wife who drew that end of the stick. She's much braver than I am."

Mr. Wright returned to the till report. "Can I help you with something?" I asked politely. "Luke mentioned you needed to review the books and inventory?"

"Yeah, just the boring stuff," he agreed. "But I can't pretend I don't love it. I love every inch of running this business."

"You must really miss it."

"I do," he sighed. "But still, it's been nice to spend more time with my wife. And I think it's been good for Luke to get out of that horrible office job he had."

"Well, what would you like me to get started with?" I asked him, moving to stand up.

"Don't get up!" he said. "There's no need!"

"That's very nice of you," I said, smiling. "But I came in today to work. So what can I help you with?"

He looked me over. "Well, it would help me a lot if you would balance the invoice book—but I'll bring it to you! You just stay right there."

He hurried off to the office and I couldn't help laughing a little. I had been expecting some business-obsessed bastard, and instead had been greeted by the nicest man alive. I could at least see where Luke got his warmth and chivalry.

Mr. Wright brought out the invoice book and we both set to work. Occasionally he would ask me a question, but mostly we worked in companionable silence. After half an hour or so, I went to unlock the front door. We had several customers right away, so I stayed busy. I kept glancing at my watch, expecting Luke at any minute.

"He must have really had a rough night," Mr. Wright said, catching me checking the time again.

"I guess so," I agreed. "He hadn't been out with his friends in a while. I think they got carried away."

"Yes; from what I hear he's spending most of his time with you," he said, grinning.

I blushed.

"He's a good boy," Mr. Wright said seriously. "I hope he's being good to you."

"He's very nice to me," I assured him, embarrassed but rather touched.

"Good! Has he cooked for you yet?"

"Um, yeah, he has," I said, uncertainly. Would that make his dad mad? But Mr. Wright just smiled.

"He's a wonderful cook, isn't he?" he asked.

Well, that was unexpected. I thought his parents didn't approve of Luke's culinary passion.

"He always talked about going to culinary school," Mr. Wright continued, oblivious to my confusion. "But when the time came he said he would rather bum around Europe for a while and learn that way. His mother and I had to get pretty firm with him in the end. I told him if he was serious about cooking as a career he should get a solid background in business. That way he could run his own restaurant, and not be at the whim of some manager."

I was very confused now. This was a very different version of the events. Had I misunderstood something?

"When he finished we offered to pay his way through his culinary classes, but he refused. He really had his heart set on going to Europe. I can't say I blame him, and Luke's always been very stubborn about these kinds of things." Mr. Wright was babbling on now, in the way that parents often do when they're undeniably proud of their children.

Instinctively, I believed him. I couldn't imagine why Luke would have lied to me about this, but I knew I trusted Mr. Wright's version of the events.

We were incredibly slow that afternoon. Jack showed up, per usual, and I found myself with very little to do and way too much to think about. About an hour before my shift was scheduled to end, Luke still hadn't shown up. "Mr. Wright," I said timidly. "Since we're so slow, would you mind terribly if I head home for the day?"

"Not at all, Ginny," he said, patting me on the back. "You must be so tired. I don't know how you young women do it."

I shook his hand and told him it had been nice to meet him, then hurried out to my car. I had a horrible suspicion that Luke would arrive at any minute and, for the first time since we had met, I had no desire to see him.

Chapter Twenty-six

Over the next few weeks, I tried to put my afternoon with Mr. Wright out of my head. I knew I should bring it up with Luke, ask him what the hell was going on, but I just couldn't summon the energy to do so. Instead I let it slide, let things continue on as they had been.

I was seeing my doctor every other week now. The baby was growing just as he should, and, if his kicking was anything to judge by, he was getting stronger by the day. My weight was increasing, too: I had put on nearly thirty pounds. I had always been a pretty slim girl—running track had helped—so my new body was completely astonishing to me.

Jen was now bugging me, on a daily basis, to "prepare for the baby." I wasn't exactly sure what she meant by that, but I kept assuring her I was on top of things. We did sit down with Annie one day early in June to pack my hospital bag—I told Jen it was way too soon, but she warned me I could go into early labor any time. The girls helped me pack my cutest pajamas, some books, a robe, and my toiletries. No matter how much I procrastinated, the baby's arrival was getting closer every day.

After we finished packing, Annie left to go to work—she was stage managing a show downtown, but had a backup in place in case I went into labor during the show's run. Jen had a date that night so I followed her into her room to help her get ready.

"You look pretty," I told her wistfully, as she curled her dark hair into a sleek bob.

"Thank you, sweetie," she said, misting her head with hair spray.

Jen reached into her jewelry box and pulled out a thin silver chain. "No, no," I instructed. "Here, can I pick it?"

"Sure," she said, moving aside.

I rooted around until I found what I wanted—a large coral pendant on a chunky silver chain. "You need something bolder, to pop against your dress," I explained as I fastened it around her neck. "There, that looks awesome together."

Jen looked at herself in the full length mirror behind her door. She was wearing a simple black shift with thigh high suede boots. Elegant, but plain. The necklace added just the right touch, if I do say so myself.

"You're right. Thanks, hon." She smiled at me.

"I have to live vicariously through you," I said with a sigh. "It's my only enjoyment these days."

"Give me a break," she said. "You have the cutest boyfriend any of us have ever had. Vicariously my ass."

"You owe me fifty cents," I told her. "And yes, I may have a cute boyfriend, but I'm the size of a house. Dressing up and looking all cute are out for me now."

"Perhaps," she said, gathering up her purse and a sweater. "But he's crazy about you anyhow. That has to count for something."

I kissed her cheek as she left, then wandered aimlessly around the empty house. Between the girls trying to keep me company, and my recent time with Luke, it had been a while since I had spent much time here alone.

I ended up sitting at the desk in my bedroom. I hadn't looked inside the lowest drawer in several months. I didn't like to think about the things I had put there. But tonight, I took a deep breath and pulled it open.

There was the envelope, the one from Josh. Inside the envelope was the cash from his parents. I hadn't used it, of course. I didn't want their money. I didn't want them to have anything to do with my life. But I never returned it either. When push came to shove, the most important thing in my life was this baby. If there was ever an emergency, if there was ever something that I couldn't deal with, I would never forgive myself if I gave up the only source of money we had to help us.

I pulled out the envelope and turned it over in my hands. I hadn't looked at it since that day Annie read it aloud to us. Hearing it once was enough for me. If I closed my eyes I could remember so clearly the pain of that day, of hearing what Josh had done to me. I rubbed my belly, trying to keep the baby calm as my heart started racing. I hadn't let myself think about Josh in so long...

*   *   *

It was January, cold outside and snowing. Josh would be leaving for London in two days. I had wanted to spend this night with him, just the two of us, but he had work to do at the magazine. I paced through our tiny, silent apartment, trying to quash the rising panic that seemed always just below the surface now.

What was I going to do when Josh left? How would I occupy my time? Two months was so long. We hadn't been apart for more than a few days in all the time we had spent together. I tried to picture myself here, in this apartment, without him, and I couldn't. The very thought made me feel so nervous I wanted to climb out of my skin. Suddenly, I had to get away.

I bundled up in my winter things and headed out into the cold, catching the bus that would take me toward campus. I knew there were at least two good parties going on tonight, and I would simply stop at the first one I came to.

The house was crammed with people. I didn't recognize more than one or two, but I decided it hardly mattered. I didn't plan on being in conversation mode for long. I made a beeline to the keg and downed my first cup in two gulps. As I filled my second, I caught sight of someone staring at me from across the room.

His name was Jeremy. He was cute, in a nondescript sort of way. He had brought a bottle of vodka, and he offered me a shot. I figured shots would get me where I wanted to be a hell of a lot quicker than beer, so I followed him upstairs into one of the bedrooms. It was a typical frat house and I tried to ignore the dirty clothes on the floor and the stink of smoke that permeated the air.

Jeremy and I talked about music. His taste was pretty good actually, and the more I drank the more interesting he became to me. The last I could remember, we had pounded five shots each. The fact that everything after is a blank told me that we didn't stop there.

The next thing I knew, a bright light was shining in my face. I opened my eyes groggily and tried to make out where I was. I was naked and laying under a sheet, but I knew this wasn't my bed. There was someone next to me, and I realized with horror that it was not Josh. Where was I?

"Ginny?" It was Josh's voice, Josh was here, somewhere. But not in bed with me? I couldn't figure out what was going on. What was that light? Where was Josh?

I tried to wipe the blurriness out of my eyes as I peered toward the bright light that had woken me. Oh, of course, it was the doorway, and the light was coming in from the hall. "Ginny?" I heard again, and suddenly, I understood. That blur there in the light— that was Josh. Josh was standing in the doorway, looking at me, watching me. And I was naked, in bed with another man.

Chapter Twenty-seven

I wiped at the tears running down my cheeks. "Mommy really messed up, baby," I whispered, rubbing my belly gently. "This all might have been so different for you." I felt a sob rise in my throat, and I didn't bother to muffle it. There was no one to hear me, no one but my baby.

"I'm so sorry, sweetie," I gulped. "This whole thing was my fault. Your daddy was not a bad guy. I drove him away from us because I broke his heart." The baby, responding to my voice, started kicking, and I cried harder. I wanted Josh here. He should be experiencing this with me. His decision to not be involved had destroyed me, it had hurt me to my core. But really, how could I blame him? Of course he didn't want to be tied to me.

Josh, amazingly, didn't dump me right away after he found me at that party. We spent the next two days holed up in our apartment, crying and arguing. He was furious with me, of course, but he still loved me. I couldn't tell him for sure what had happened, because I didn't remember any of it. Josh conceded that things had been difficult for us for a long time, and he was willing to put off any major decisions for the time being.

So I helped him pack and he headed off to London, telling me he thought it would be good for us to be apart while we thought things through. I missed him the entire time he was gone, but I dreaded when he would return. Surely he would end things with me then. I spent most nights alone in our apartment, drinking until I could sleep.

Josh came home in March. He told me he had missed me and he wanted to make things work. I prayed with every fiber of my being that things could go back to the way they had been. But of course, they never would. We fought. It seemed like we fought all the time. I was jealous, possessive. He was alternately angry and weary, so tired of the drama. We lasted another three months, but as graduation drew closer, we both knew it was over.

Josh was the one who finally ended it, officially. He told me that he loved me but he just couldn't do it anymore. He said that as long as I refused to create a life of my own we would just keep coming back to the same problems. He forgave me for what I had done with that guy, because he knew, better than anyone else ever had, that it wasn't me. Not really. But he just couldn't do it anymore.

I cried. I begged him to change his mind. I told him I would do whatever he wanted, be whoever he wanted.

He told me that was the problem.

In a horrible last-ditch attempt, I told him I thought I might be pregnant. I burn with shame just thinking about saying those words to him. It didn't work, of course. He just looked at me and told me that if I was pregnant he would help me, but it would make him very, very sad.

That's why I could never tell him about the baby. That's why I tried to keep it a secret for so long. I couldn't bear the thought of telling him and knowing it would make him miserable. I couldn't bear the thought of hurting him anymore.

*   *   *

I didn't read the letter from Josh that night. I figured I had spent enough time walking down memory lane. It wouldn't get me anywhere. I had good things in my life now. The baby would be here soon. I needed to keep moving on.

I went back downstairs and decided I would make myself an ice cream sundae and curl up in front of a mindless movie. As I headed into the kitchen, my phone rang. It was Luke.

"Ginny," he said, his voice low and excited. "Can I see you?"

"Now?" I asked, looking at the clock. It was nearly ten and I was already in my pajamas.

"I have something to tell you!" he replied. "Please, it won't take long."

"Sure. Come on over."

I hung up my phone and headed to the bathroom. I washed my face, trying to erase any sign of tears, and brushed my hair for good measure. Luke must have been on his way when he called, because I heard a knock on the front door after only a few minutes.

Luke pulled me into a hug the second I opened the door. "I have great news!"

"What's up?" I asked, smiling at his obvious excitement.

"I have the money now!"

I stared at him blankly. I had no idea what he was talking about.

"For the Europe trip!" he added.

"Oh," I said slowly. "I didn't realize you were still saving for that..."

"I wasn't," he said quickly. "All the money was just sitting there in my account. But I just got a call from my broker; something awesome happened. One of my investments went big this afternoon. He just got the numbers in. It's a windfall—way more than enough to go!"

It probably should have told me something that my first thought was for his father, not for me. "What about the store, Luke?"

"What about it?" he said, a touch of petulance in his voice. "It's not my store."

"Yeah, but your dad relies on you. He can't work."

"He can afford to hire someone else to run the damn thing for him. It's not my problem anymore." Luke definitely sounded petulant now, childish almost. The word selfish sprang to mind, but I tried to quash it back down. This wasn't my fight.

"Well, I think that's great for you. I know how much you wanted this."

"It's not just for me, Ginny!" he said, the excitement back. "It's for both of us!"

It was silent for a moment. "I don't understand."

"I'm telling you that I want you to come with me."

I stared at him in disbelief. "What?"

"I want you to come with me. To Spain. And whatever comes after."

Wait...what? "Luke...I can't come with you. I'm having a baby in a month."

"I realize that, Ginny," he said, rolling his eyes. "He would come with us. The three of us."

"I can't do that," I said, shaking my head. This was absurd.

"Why not? It would be amazing! You and me, the baby, traveling around, seeing the world. What could be better than that?"

"I can't have a newborn baby on the road with me...it's ridiculous."

"Ginny, you've said yourself you didn't want to be stuck here forever. You've always wanted to travel. You want to see the world! Don't you want that for your baby, too?"

Of course I wanted to see the world, and of course I wanted my baby to have amazing experiences...but there was something wrong here, something I couldn't put my finger on.

"Luke," I began slowly. "I never said that. I never said I didn't want to be stuck here." Yes, that's what was bothering me. He had said that, many times, but I never had. "I like it here. I like my life, my friends, my job...this is where I want to have my baby."

He stared at me, aghast. "You want to stay here? In Michigan? This is where you want to live your life?"

"Yeah. It is."

"Like, forever?" he asked in disbelief.

He looked so sad I considered taking it back—but only for a split-second. Luke was not my life. I wasn't going to follow him, I wasn't going to hide from my problems with him. Maybe a year ago, I would have. But Jen was right: I had changed. I was a different person. I wasn't that girl that went out to find approval in men because she was lonely. I wasn't that girl that needed alcohol or parties or sex to make me feel good about myself. And I didn't need to follow a man around on his adventures in order to be happy. I had my own life.

"I can't believe this," he muttered. "I can't believe you'd try to hold me back like this."

"Wait—what?"

"It's just like my parents. They never cared about what I wanted either." There was a bitter expression on Luke's face. The word 'childish' sprang to mind again. He looked exactly like a little boy who wasn't getting his way. Like a kid who would try to make his mom feel guilty in order to get what he wanted.

"What are you talking about?"

"I told you what they did, Ginny, how they refused to let me go to culinary school. Don't you see that this is what I need to do?"

"I *do* see that." I was starting to feel very impatient now. "But, Luke, your dad told me they *were* willing to let you go to school, but you refused unless they would send you to Europe."

"And you believed that? Figures!"

177

I stared at him in disbelief. This was like a completely different person. A demanding, childish, temperamental person.

But on second thought, maybe this reaction did kind of make sense. Throughout the course of our relationship, Luke had been accustomed to getting exactly what he wanted. He saw me whenever he wanted, he chose our activities and meals, I helped him with all the things he hated to do in the store. He was charming, sure, and treated me great—but he also basked in my praise, in my obvious gratitude.

Looking at him now, I wondered if I knew him at all.

An argument sprang to my tongue—he was being ridiculous, I had no intention of holding him back, et cetera. But suddenly, it didn't matter to me anymore. This was going nowhere. What was the point of dragging it out any further?

"I'm sorry, Luke," I said softly. "You've been amazing to me, and I've really enjoyed being with you...I just think we're in two totally different places right now."

A flicker of shock crossed his features, but it was quickly replaced by an expressionless mask. "You're ending this? Just like that?"

"I think it's the right thing to do."

He nodded, refusing to meet my eyes. "I think you're right." So quickly I might have imagined it he leaned forward, kissed my cheek, and turned. He was gone before I could say a word.

Chapter Twenty-eight

When I told her what I had done, Annie was aghast.

"You have got to be kidding me," she said, her eyes open wide. "Seriously, Ginny, tell me you're kidding."

"Sorry, Ann," I said, shrugging my shoulders. "It's over." We were sitting in the living room on Sunday morning, waiting for Jen to wake up and, hopefully, make us some breakfast.

"Ginny," Annie said slowly. "The most gorgeous man *we have ever seen* asked you to go to Europe, indefinitely, free of charge. And you turned him down?"

"Annie, I'm having a baby in two months," I said. "Do you really think it would have been wise to go running off with a man I've been dating for eight weeks? To leave the country with a newborn baby?"

"I guess not," she sighed. "But God, Ginny...he was so pretty!"

"I know," I replied. "But I wasn't in love with him."

"What's love matter when you look like that?" she demanded.

"It matters a lot when you're talking about a baby," I said seriously. "This is real life, Annie."

"What's real life?" Jen appeared in the doorway, wrapping her robe around herself as she yawned.

"Ginny broke up with the hot man," Annie said solemnly.

"I didn't really break up with him," I said. "I just told him I didn't want to go to Europe with him...we kind of agreed on the breaking up part."

"Okay, back up," Jen said, holding up her hands. "Start over."

"Why don't you make us some food and she can tell you all about it?" Annie said innocently.

"Fine," Jen laughed, heading into the kitchen as Annie and I followed her. Annie made coffee and Jen started cracking eggs while I sat in a kitchen chair and told her everything.

"Wow," Jen said when I had finished. "So he's just going to leave the store and take off? That's rough for his dad."

"I know," I said.

"It seems a little...selfish."

"That's exactly what I thought," I nodded.

"I don't think it's selfish to do what you've always wanted to do," Annie said. "I mean, you said this was his dream, why shouldn't he do it?"

"I'm not saying he shouldn't go," I said. "But taking off without warning...it just seems like he's leaving his dad in the lurch." I considered telling them the rest, the way that Luke had lied to me, and then acted when I called him on it...but I felt tired of the whole situation. What was the point in reliving it all?

"Well, I think you made the right choice," Jen said as she slid omelets off the griddle onto our plates. I grabbed the juice and the three of us sat at the kitchen table. I noticed Annie wasn't meeting my eyes.

"Okay, spill it," I demanded.

"What?" she asked innocently.

"You clearly disapprove, so just tell me what you're thinking."

"I just...I can't help but wonder..."

"*What*, Annie?"

"I can't help but wonder if this isn't about Josh," she admitted. "I think you're still hoping he's going to change his mind and come back, and you don't want to be in Europe with another man when that happens."

I stared at her, feeling slightly offended. "It's not about Josh," I said quietly. "It's about my baby. I'm not going to go running around a foreign country with a newborn just because it might be romantic and fun. I want to have this baby here, where my friends are, where my home is. I have a job I love for the first time in my life. I feel stable...I feel good. And I don't want to give that up for a guy, even if he is, admittedly, quite hot. Is that so hard to believe?"

Annie was staring at me, a weird expression on her face, "No," she said softly. "It's not hard at all."

I looked over at Jen, who was also regarding me with a strange look. "Okay, what, you guys? You're both looking at me all weird."

"We're just proud of you, that's all," Jen said, smiling.

"Yeah, you sound like a mom," Annie agreed.

"Well," I said, spearing a piece of omelet with my fork, "I guess I'm starting to feel like one."

* * *

I was not looking forward to going to work the next day. I had texted Luke several times on Sunday afternoon, but thus far he had ignored me. I was anticipating a day of awkwardness when I got to the store.

What I was not expecting was to see Luke's dad, again behind the counter.

"Mr. Wright," I said in surprise. "I wasn't expecting you today!"

He sighed, and he looked much more tired than he had the last time I saw him.

Suddenly, it dawned on me. "Luke left already, didn't he?"

Mr. Wright nodded. "Last night," he said. "He came to the house in the afternoon with his bags all packed and told us he was leaving."

I had to sit down. I couldn't believe that Luke would leave so quickly, without saying goodbye. "He didn't tell you?" Mr. Wright asked sharply.

"He told me he was going, I just didn't know when."

He shook his head. "That's horrible, Ginny. I'm so sorry."

I shrugged. "I guess he just figured we said everything there was to say."

Beyond the surprise, I wasn't quite sure how I felt. What I had told Annie was true: I wasn't in love with Luke. But he had been kind to me, and he was fun to be with. And he wanted me, even though I was seven months pregnant and getting bigger by the day. I would miss him.

But I was still glad I had decided to stay.

"You've done a great job here," Mr. Wright was saying. "I'm hoping you'll want to stay even though Luke is gone."

"Of course I do!" I was shocked he would think otherwise. "Mr. Wright, I love this store. This is my favorite job I've ever had!"

"Oh good," he said with relief. "I would have hated to lose you. I've been looking over all of the paperwork—Luke was giving you a lot of responsibility, wasn't he?"

I shrugged. "I offered a lot, I don't mind office work."

"And this promotional campaign that did so well last month, the packaging of paperbacks with vouchers from the coffee shop down the street—that was your idea, wasn't it?"

"Well, I always notice people sitting over there reading, it seemed like a natural combination."

"You have a good head for this stuff, Ginny," he said seriously. "I think you'd make a great manager."

"Really?" I was immensely pleased.

He nodded. "Look, I know you have a lot on your plate, with the baby coming and all—but what would you think about giving it a try?"

"Managing? For real?"

"I think you'd be great," he said. "We could start you off part-time until the baby comes, give you a chance to get your feet wet—that way I could be in a few days a week and my wife wouldn't have to kill me for working too much." He winked at me. "Then, after your maternity leave, you could come back and manage full-time."

I was speechless. This was perfect, the absolute perfect opportunity for me. "I would love to," I said, trying to keep my voice from shaking. "Mr. Wright, I would really love to."

I couldn't believe my good luck—except it wasn't really luck, was it? For once in my life I was working hard, and I was making good choices. And it was starting to pay off for me, and for my baby.

Chapter Twenty-nine

Thirty-six Weeks*: You're nearly there now! In just one short week you will be considered full term, at which point the baby could be born at any time! Now is the time to do all those last minute things that you may have been putting off. Is the nursery decorated? Your hospital bag packed? Do you have your crib, your stroller, your bassinet, your car seat? The list goes on and on! Most women enjoy this aspect of upcoming birth—chances are you've been shopping for weeks! That's great news: you'll be all ready when the baby comes, giving you the opportunity to relax and enjoy your little one!—Dr. Rebecca Carr, A Gal's Guide to a Fabulous First Pregnancy!*

"Ginny," Jen asked cautiously. "What exactly are you doing?"

"What does it look like I'm doing?" I muttered. I was kneeling on the kitchen floor, scrubbing the linoleum.

"Okay," she said. "Maybe I should ask *why* are you cleaning the kitchen floor at seven thirty on Saturday morning?"

"Because the kitchen floor is filthy," I replied. "Look at it! When's the last time we cleaned it?"

"I'm not sure," she said, in that same cautious voice, as if she were addressing a crazy woman and not her best friend.

"Look, Jen," I said, leaning back on my feet and blowing the hair off my forehead. "This entire house is filthy, and there's going to be a baby here soon. Would you want your baby crawling around on this floor?"

"You have a point," she conceded. "But I don't think your baby is going to be crawling any time soon."

I rolled my eyes and went back to my scrubbing.

"Just be careful, okay?" Jen said. "You don't want to throw your back out or anything."

"I'm fine," I replied, as Jen started to edge out of the room.

"Oh, and don't forget," she called over her shoulder. "Annie and I are taking you out to lunch today, and we're not taking no for an answer."

Annie and Jen had been bugging me about spending an afternoon together for a few weeks. I think they were worried about me being lonely after Luke. I did miss him, but it certainly wasn't heartbreaking. I was staying pretty busy with work: Mr. Wright had let me take some shifts as manager and I loved it. It was challenging, but fun. And it felt really good to know I was doing something productive, something that would help my baby.

After I finished the floor, I decided the fridge could do with cleaning out. Then I dusted all the furniture and vacuumed. When Annie woke up at ten thirty, she stared at me in confusion for a full minute before declaring that I was nuts and walking off to make herself breakfast.

At eleven thirty, Jen cornered me in the bathroom and demanded that I drop my scrub brush. "You need to get ready," she told me firmly.

"Jen, can't I finish this room first? It's only lunch, it can wait a while."

"Nope," she said. "We made reservations at a nice place. We're going to put on cute clothes and go out and have a nice lunch. Now get moving."

"But look at this grout!" I exclaimed. "Jen, it's awful!"

"Ginny," she said patiently. "This is called nesting. It's very normal. Your hormones are telling you to get ready for the baby, and that's fine. But I don't have time for it this afternoon. Now please get your ass up off the floor and get ready." She forcibly pulled the scrub brush from my hands and picked up my bucket. "Now, Ginny."

I sighed and did as she asked, not even bothering to collect my fifty cents. I took a nice warm shower then headed up to my room, where Jen had laid out a cute sundress for me. I figured that was taking her control freak tendencies a little too far, but I didn't feel like arguing so I put the dress on. I curled my hair and put some makeup on, beginning to get into the spirit of things.

That is, until I tried to put on my shoes.

Annie found me five minutes later, sitting on the floor of my bedroom, shoes spread all around me, sobbing uncontrollably. "What's wrong with you?" she cried in dismay.

"I wanted...to look...cute!" I wailed, as Annie gingerly patted my back. "But none...none of my shoes fit...because *I'm too fat!*"

To her credit, Annie managed to not laugh at me, or even mention the word hormones. Instead, she rubbed my back until I calmed down a little, and then convinced me to come down to her room and borrow some heels from her. Her feet, as she pointed out reasonably, were two sizes bigger than mine and should fit much better.

Ten minutes later, with a pair of Annie's wedge sandals strapped firmly on my feet, and my make-up freshly reapplied, we were finally ready to leave. The three of us piled into Jen's Jeep and headed downtown. "Where are we going, anyways?" I asked.

"It's a surprise," Annie said mysteriously as Jen turned up the radio, effectively ending all conversation.

We ended up in Midtown. Jen pulled right up to a gorgeous mansion, parking in the valet lane and handing her keys off to the young man who had appeared at her window.

We climbed out of the car and I clapped my hands. "Are we eating at the Whitney?" I asked excitedly.

"That we are!" Jen said, linking her arm through mine and steering me into the building.

The Whitney was a gorgeous old mansion built in the late 1890s and converted into a very swanky restaurant. I had always wanted to eat there, ever since I was a little girl, but it had never been in my budget.

"Thank you, girls!" I cried.

"Well, we knew you always wanted to come here," Annie said, smiling at me. "You've been working so hard, we figured it would be a nice treat."

As we entered the opulent lobby, I felt giddy with excitement. It was so beautiful inside, just like I had imagined. I drank in the wood paneling, elaborate moldings, stained glass, and lush carpets. I was in heaven and we'd barely crossed the threshold.

Jen stepped up to the desk and spoke quietly with the hostess, who smiled at us and gestured that we should follow her.

She led us up a sweeping staircase to the second floor. "You ladies will be in the Flora Tea Room," she said, smiling over her shoulder. We walked down a short hallway and then stopped at the entrance to the tea room.

As the hostess stepped out of the way, I gasped. Gathered around the entrance were thirty or so people—all of whom I knew. Girls from high school and college, my old track friends, Annie's and Jen's moms, various aunts and cousins, Beth from the bookstore—and my mother.

Jen leaned into me. "Welcome to your baby shower," she whispered.

*　*　*

It was the best afternoon I could have imagined.

After we entered the room, I promptly burst into tears—of course. "You can't surprise a pregnant lady like that!" I wailed, as Annie hugged me and laughed. I was passed around the room, hugging everyone. I couldn't believe so many people were here, that so many of them wanted to support me.

The biggest surprise was my mother. She showed not a trace of embarrassment or disapproval, merely pulling me in for a rare hug and whispering that I looked beautiful. As I pulled away from her, I thought I may have even seen a trace of tears around her eyes.

Annie and Jen had planned several cheesy games, which, they assured me, were essential to the mom-to-be experience. The games mostly seemed designed to embarrass me: everyone had to guess the size of my belly, guess how many baby items I could correctly name, and blindfolded, tape a paper baby on my belly. Then there was something disgusting involving melting candy bars in diapers—I had to leave the room for that one.

After the games we ate a lovely meal: tomato bisque, bruschetta, chicken piccata, and some kind of stuffed eggplant dish. It was delicious. When we finished eating, the staff brought out my cake. It was a simple sheet cake, iced in a delicate blue shade. The decorations were minimal; just a sprinkling of silver stars around the corners. In the center of the cake, in dark blue script, was the phrase, "A Precious Gift from Heaven... Congratulations, Ginny!" I cried some more—then ate three pieces.

When the food had been cleared, the wait staff brought out tea and Jen marched me to the front of the room, where she sat me in an elegant cushioned chair. It was only then that I noticed the stack of presents in the corner.

Two days ago I had worried that I would never have the money to afford everything the baby needed—now I wondered where I would put it all. Jen admitted to me later that she had registered for me, so everyone invited would know what I needed. The baby now had his car seat, a darling white bassinette, a plastic bath, vast amounts of clothes, towels and blankets, even a jogging stroller (a joint gift from my track friends).

My mother, to my never-ending surprise, outdid them all: she and my dad had signed me up for a year's worth of home delivery cloth diaper service. "I know you worry about all that environmental stuff," she explained sheepishly. I had, in fact, gone through a militant-environmental phase as a teenager, mostly to annoy her. I was touched beyond belief that she had remembered.

Jen and Annie's gifts were last. They shyly presented me with a bedding set almost identical to the one we had seen that day at Baby and Me!—not only the blanket I had seen Jen working on, but matching sheets, pillows and a bed skirt. I was speechless. "We both did the sewing," Jen said. "Annie was really good with the pillows." Thinking of the two of them—the least domestic girls I knew—sitting up late at night sewing for me—it made my eyes well with tears all over again.

"We got you one other thing," Annie said, reaching behind the table to pull out a gift bag. "We figured most of your gifts would be for the baby. This one is just for you." From the bag I pulled out a tube of Victoria's Secret body lotion, a set of silky pajamas, bath oils, slippers, a massive box of Godiva chocolates, and a bottle of pinot grigio—"To celebrate not being pregnant anymore," Annie explained.

I looked around at all the people who loved me, who loved my baby. Especially Annie and Jen. I was absolutely overwhelmed with their kindness and generosity. Since I couldn't think of the words to tell them how much it all meant to me, and my throat was feeling tight with tears yet again, I decided to keep it simple.

"Thank you."

Chapter Thirty

Later that night I sat with Annie and Jen in our living room. We had hauled all the presents inside and piled them up in the corner of our seldom-used dining room. Jen insisted that I wash all the new baby clothes—she had read that it was important in one of the baby books. I wondered, not for the first time, just how much research she was putting into this whole thing.

We had washed and folded all the tiny pieces (I couldn't stop myself from cooing over each one, though Annie gave me several despairing looks), put together the bassinet, assembled the bouncy chair, and tried to figure out what, exactly, the diaper genie was supposed to do. I was bone tired, and, for once, the girls were even worse. I couldn't get over how much effort and expense they had put into this day for me.

"I want to cook you guys dinner," I said impulsively, standing up and stretching.

"Why?" The alarm in Annie's voice was undeniable, which I found slightly offensive.

"Because you worked so hard on this shower," I said. "You guys look exhausted; I want you to sit and rest."

193

"That's nice," Jen said uncertainly. "What...ah...are you going to make?"

"You guys!" I said, irritated, "I am not that bad a cook!"

"Of course you're not, hon," Jen said, shooting Annie a warning look. "But you've had a big day, too. Why don't we just order in?"

I thought about that for a moment. I could head into the kitchen and try to scrounge something up, more than likely burning it, or I could pick up the phone.

"Okay," I said quickly. "But I'm buying."

We opted for Thai food, primarily because they delivered and none of us felt like going out again. Instead, we slipped into our PJs and stretched out on the couches, while we ate straight from the cartons.

"We really need to figure out this name thing," Annie said, in between bites.

I sighed. "Nothing feels right," I told them. "I'm hoping something will jump out at me once I see him."

"Don't you think that's a pretty risky strategy?" Jen asked. "What if nothing comes to you? Do you really want everyone referring to him as 'Baby Boy McKensie' for the first few days of his life?"

I laughed. "Fair point. Alright, let's try to figure this out."

"I'll grab my laptop. There are tons of baby name websites!" Jen said excitedly, jumping up and heading to her bedroom. I rolled my eyes at Annie.

"She's probably been dying to do this for weeks," she muttered.

Jen returned and quickly booted up her computer while Annie and I gathered around her. Within seconds she had pulled up a site. "Did you actually have that saved under your favorites?" Annie asked. "God, what a nerd."

Jen started reading down the list. It was pretty overwhelming. There were modern names, ethnic names, popular names, quirky names. "Holy crap," Anne muttered. "There's thousands of names on here!"

"Well, what direction do you want to take, Gin?" Jen asked. "Popular, old fashioned, something a little different?"

"Um..." I had no idea. This was much harder than I thought it would be. "Let's start with popular names."

"Good idea," Annie agreed. "Then he won't get picked on in school for having a freak name."

"Okay, let's see...Aidan is very popular right now...then there's Levi, Tyler, Noah, Jackson, Jayden...any of these jumping out at you?"

"I can't picture you with a baby named Jayden," Annie said, squinting her eyes. "Too trendy."

"Wanna try some celebrity baby names?" Jen asked.

"Sure." She clicked on the screen and a new list came up.

"Hmm...we've got Wynn, Satchel, Coco, Lyric, Moxie, Apple..."

"Okay, that's enough of that!" Annie demanded. "You cannot name your baby any of these! You're not trendy or quirky. You're classic."

I smiled, taking that as a compliment.

"She has a point. You're not really a 'Lyric' kind of mom," Jen agreed.

"You could always go back to names from books," Annie said. "Like you were gonna do if it was a girl."

I thought about that, but there weren't too many male names I loved from literature. "What about Holden?" Jen asked. "That's from a book. Or Jem—you liked *To Kill a Mockingbird*, didn't you? Or there's...hmm, who was the guy Anne Shirley got with?"

"Gilbert," I said automatically. *Anne of Green Gables* was probably my all-time favorite book.

"Nope!" Annie exclaimed. "Gilbert, Jem, and Holden are not classic. What's wrong with something simple? Like Thomas, or Michael, or Daniel?"

Daniel. Danny. Just like Josh's dream.

"Daniel..." Jen said slowly, thinking it over. "You know what, I really like it!"

"Yeah, I can see you with a Daniel," Annie said.

I could see it too. If I was honest with myself, every time I pictured the baby, it's what I thought of: that image Josh had imparted all those years ago. Our baby, Danny. But did I want to keep that connection alive? Would it make me sad to look at that baby, the baby we had dreamed of, and know that Josh didn't want it?

I didn't feel sad now, thinking about it. I felt...right. I'm ashamed to admit it, but I *wanted* that attachment to Josh, even now, even after everything. If he wouldn't be in our lives, this could be one tiny way the baby could be connected to his father, to the very best memory I had of our relationship.

"Daniel," I said out loud. "Danny...I like it too."

Annie and Jen squealed and hugged me. "Baby Danny!" Jen exclaimed. "It's perfect!"

And in that moment, I really felt like it was.

Chapter Thirty-one

Thirty-eight Weeks: Congratulations! You have nearly crossed the finish line. Though your due date is still a few weeks off, keep in mind that you could go into labor at any time. In the last thirty-eight weeks you have probably gained at least twenty-five pounds. Your baby weighs anywhere from five to eight pounds! You may be feeling achy, bloated, hot and uncomfortable, but inside your womb your baby is perfect! All of his features and organs are fully formed—he's just waiting to meet you!—Dr. Rebecca Carr, A Gal's Guide to a Fabulous First Pregnancy!

The third Friday in July was one of the hottest afternoons of the summer. Annie arrived home after her classes to find me stretched out on the couch in nothing but a pair of old boxer shorts and a bathing suit cover up. The combination of my expanding girth and the extreme heat had led me to seek refuge inside, with all the curtains closed, the lights off, my feet in a bucket of water and an oscillating fan targeted straight at my face.

"You are a classy-looking babe, Ginny McKensie," Annie pronounced as she set her bag down and slipped out of her flip flops.

"I do my best," I said.

"Have you been sitting here all day?"

I had stopped working that Wednesday. The Wrights were generously granting me two full months of maternity leave. I think they were probably just terrified I would go into labor in the store. It was good to have some time off before the baby came, particularly as it was getting harder to do essential things—like get dressed or, you know, walk.

"I haven't moved since eleven a.m.," I replied. "Now be quiet, please; talking makes me too hot."

"Ginny, you have the air cranked up and a fan blowing on your face. How are you still hot?"

"Um, I don't know, Ann, maybe it's the fact that I'm growing a human being, I'm roughly the size of a hippo, and it's ninety-five degrees out."

"Good point." Annie plopped on the recliner next to me and put her feet up. "God, I'm tired," she moaned. "I taught four classes this afternoon."

"Well, join me in my lovely land of laziness; it's a wonderful place."

Shortly after Ann arrived, my cell phone rang. I looked down at the screen, groaned, and hit the ignore button. "You're not gonna answer that?" Annie asked.

"Nope."

"Why not?"

"Because it's my mother, and if I talk to her right now, I think my head might explode."

My mother had taken our semi-reconciliation at the shower as a cue to try and get involved in every aspect of my pregnancy. Over the last few weeks we had had several maddening conversations about my health, the baby's health, what I was eating, how much I was sleeping, where I was going to get the baby baptized. A few of these had ended in shouting matches, and I was not eager to go there right now.

Jen arrived home about an hour later. As she opened the door and the outside light filtered in around her, I gasped and held up my hands.

"Light bad," I moaned. "Close it, close it!"

Jen shut the door and looked around the dark room.

"What on earth are you guys doing?" she asked, wrinkling her nose.

"Ginny is hot and uncomfortable, due to her massive knocked-up-ness," Annie explained drowsily. "I have joined her in her efforts to beat the heat to show my support."

"She says she's being supportive," I complained. "But she refuses to get up to get me more iced tea."

"You guys," Jen said patiently. "It's gorgeous outside. The sun is out, there's a nice breeze. You should get out of this room, or at least open some windows, let the sun in."

"No, no, no sunlight!" I proclaimed, then groaned. "God, talking makes me *so* hot!"

"Alright, enough of this moping crap, my friends!" Jen said. "We're going out!"

"Ha!" I muttered, glaring up at her from the place I was beached on the couch. "You're a funny one, Jen Campbell."

"I'm not joking," she said firmly, walking around the room and collecting the dirty dishes I had let pile up. "This house smells. *You* are starting to smell. We need to get out."

"Jen, I'm not sure if you've noticed, but I weigh about seven hundred pounds right now. My clothes don't fit—not even the maternity ones. The only thing I can fit into is this fucking bathing suit cover up."

"Eff word!" Annie yelled, pointing at me. "You owe me a dollar."

I scowled at her.

"Ginny, who knows the next time you're going to get out of this house? We need a last night out!" Jen pleaded.

"Yeah, pretty soon your entire life is going to be poopie diapers and midnight feedings," Annie said, sounding way too gleeful for my liking.

"Careful," I warned. "I have about fifty pounds on you right now."

"And masses of dexterity and flexibility," she shot back.

"I'm not taking no for an answer," Jen said firmly, ignoring us both. "We're going out. All three of us. We're putting on cute clothes and doing our makeup and getting out of this house. Let's go."

I looked at Annie. "Jen's got her scary face on," I sighed.

"Yeah, maybe we should listen to her," she said mock-sadly.

"Oh God," I moaned. "How am I going to go out when I can't even get my ass up off the couch?"

"A-word!" Annie shouted. "You owe me fifty cents!"

Jen rolled her eyes and grabbed my arm, beginning to pull. "We'll help you. Now let's go."

* * *

We ended up at Pronto, my favorite restaurant in Royal Oak. Pronto was known for its amazing sandwiches and pasta. It had a great atmosphere; there were always interesting people, they played good music, and they housed a lively bar right next door. They also had the absolute best baked goods I have ever tasted in my life. Plus, it was well-known as a gay hangout—which we loved, as it meant cute boys to look at with no pressure to try to impress them. In other words, the perfect night out for a nine-months pregnant lady.

"Would it be rude if I drink in front of you?" Annie asked, pulling the cocktail menu to her side of the table.

"Would it stop you if I said yes?" I asked.

"Probably not," she admitted, as our waiter approached. An expert at avoiding our bickering, Jen took matters into her own hands, ordering us three identical cocktails (virgin for me). After we had placed our food orders, Jen peered at me closely.

"You know, you look pretty good tonight," she said.

"Yeah, right," I laughed. "I look like a sow."

"No really, you're pretty. Your skin is clear, your eyes are all bright. Maybe this is what they mean when they talk about a pregnant woman's glow."

"Or it just means that I live with a girl who has lots of experience in applying stage make-up," I replied.

After Jen had hauled me up off the couch they had both attacked my closet, rifling through the clothes there until they agreed on a red empire waist dress—whose hemline was, it must be said, much shorter than usual as it stretched over my gigantic belly. In fact, I had to add a pair of black leggings underneath just to make it decent to wear in public. Jen assured me it looked cute that way, and Annie pointed out that the cut accentuated my newly enhanced cleavage.

I had to admit, it had felt great to get dressed up, to have Annie do my make-up. It had been a while since we had done something fun together, just the three of us. Most of our activities and conversation now related to baby. I decided right then that tonight would be a baby-free zone.

The waiter (Jonathon, definitely gay, totally gorgeous) brought our cocktails over and Annie started telling us all about Hot Theater Tech Guy. His name was Adam, apparently, and she was pretty sure she was in love. "He's so pretty," she said dreamily. "I swear to God, exactly my type."

"Greasy and pale?" Jen asked cheerfully, making me laugh and Annie roll her eyes.

"That was one guy, God. Are you ever going to forget that?"

"No," Jen and I said in unison.

In a good mood, I decided to be nice. "What's he really like?" I asked.

She started a long monologue, detailing everything from his wiry build ("And so tall, too, mmm.") to his opinion on David Mamet plays. I tried to keep up, but I was finding that the non-alcoholic cocktail wasn't agreeing with my stomach. I pushed it aside and decided to stick with water.

"You would not believe it, guys," Annie was continuing, "he told me he felt the exact same way! I never find people in theater who think Mamet it overrated. It was like total—"

"Shit!" I interrupted, grabbing my stomach.

"What? What's wrong?" Annie was so concerned she forgot to mention the dollar penalty.

"Nothing, just some heartburn," I explained, rubbing my stomach, where the sharp pain was already dissipating.

"Are you sure?" Jen asked. They were both looking at me worriedly.

"Yeah, I'm sure. I mean, what else would it be?"

They both stared at me. "Um, well, you know, you are *pregnant*," Annie said.

"Oh come on, I'm not due for two weeks."

I was saved continuing this conversation by the arrival of our food. I tucked into my pasta—a gooey, cheesy penne concoction with grilled chicken—and ate with gusto. "Seriously," I said, almost whimpering, "this tastes even better now that I'm preg. This baby is gonna be a cheese lover, I can tell."

"Of course he is," Jen replied. "His mother is the only person I've ever known who puts cheese on apples."

"Cheese and apples," I said sternly, pointing my fork at her, "is a wonderful snack—"

Before I could finish my thought my stomach was clenched by another sharp pain. I tried not to cry out, not wanting to draw attention, but I knew the girls had noticed.

"Alright, I'm timing these now," Jen said briskly, looking down at her watch.

"Gin, were you having any of these pains earlier today?" Annie asked. "Is that part of why you were so uncomfortable?"

"I was having some *heartburn*," I said distinctly. "But it wasn't in regular intervals or anything..."

"Early contractions usually aren't regular," Jen said. "Didn't you read the baby books?"

"Yes!" I said, offended. "...Well, most of them anyhow." Annie groaned. "What? I have like two weeks left to learn everything I need to know about labor. I'm fine!" No sooner had I said this than I felt another clenching pain.

"Alright, that's it," Jen said, reaching for her purse as I clenched the table rim until my knuckles turned white. "You're having contractions and they're less than five minutes apart. That means we need to get to the hospital."

"What?" I cried, feeling panicked. "That's ridiculous! We're having dinner."

"No, Gin," Annie said, pulling her wallet out and laying down some cash. "We're having a baby. We need to go now."

They both stood, Jen reaching out to grab my hand. I pulled away from her roughly. *"No!"* I cried loudly. Most of the other diners turned in our direction. "I'm not going to the hospital! I didn't bring my hospital bag! I don't even have my trashy magazines."

"Sweetie," Jen said, crouching so she was at my eye level. "We can get you all those things. It's going to be fine." Our waiter, clearly noticing the attention we were drawing, approached our table.

"Is everything okay, ladies?" he asked.

"Oh yeah, we're fine. Our friend here is just going into labor and experiencing some denial about it," Annie said.

"I am not going into labor," I snarled.

"You see?" Annie asked the waiter, who looked downright terrified.

"Ginny," Jen tried again. "I doubt this nice man wants you to go into labor in his restaurant. How about we take off and get you to the hospital?"

"Yeah, think of the panic you'll cause the gay boys at the bar next door if you show your vagina in here," Annie added.

"Do you have to make jokes right now?" Jen hissed. "Can't you see how terrified she is?" Jen again leaned down to my level, squeezing my hands as she moved her face closer to mine and spoke to me in a voice you might use to talk a crazy person down from the ledge. "Maybe you're right. Maybe it's not time for the baby. But I still think we should go see your doctor and make sure, okay?"

My heart was racing by now and I could feel my breathing coming in sharp gasps. I couldn't be having the baby yet, I just couldn't. I wasn't ready. "Ginny," Jen said quietly, and I looked into her calm, familiar eyes.

"Okay," I whispered. "Let's go."

Chapter Thirty-two

My first impression of the hospital was noise. Noise and light.

Jen, for all her calm in the restaurant, drove like a maniac to get us to the emergency room. In the car, Annie kept up a steady stream of ill-timed jokes, which I assumed were meant to mask her nerves. For my part, I tried to pretend I was anywhere else. Talk about denial.

Annie's cool, jokey demeanor wore out the second we walked through the glass double doors. "My friend's having a baby!" she shouted. "Someone help us!"

"Oh God," I muttered. "You're mortifying me."

After managing to get us both calmed down, Jen gave my information to the intake nurse. I was now settled in a bed in the maternity ward, trying my damndest not to hyperventilate as an older nurse named Tammy took my vitals and hooked me up to various monitors.

"I really don't think I'm having the baby yet," I tried to explain to her. "I'm not due for another two weeks."

"This monitor right here will track your contractions, if that's what you're having," she replied.

"And when the doctor gets here he'll measure to see if you're dilated. Then we'll know where we are, okay?"

"Sounds peachy," I muttered. Just then, another pain hit, the worst one so far. I grabbed Tammy's hand—it was the closest thing to me—and swore.

"You owe—" Annie started to say, but Jen cut her off with a shake of the head.

"We're suspending the cursing charges for the rest of the evening," she said firmly. "Ginny gets to say whatever she wants while she's in labor."

"I—am—not—in—labor!" I gasped, still clutching Tammy's hand.

"Sweetie," she murmured, brushing back my hair. "I hate to break it to you, but that was definitely a contraction. I've been doing this for thirty years. You're having a baby. Tonight."

* * *

Six hours later, I was pretty sure I was going to die.

"Annie, I think I'm going to die!" I moaned, as she wiped my forehead with a wet washcloth.

"You're not going to die," she soothed. "You're just in labor. We've discussed this. This is how it's supposed to feel."

"Then I call bullshit," I said. "I want my money back."

"Well, the next time an ex-boyfriend shows up and tries to get into your pants, remember to tell him 'no glove, no love.'"

"Words cannot begin to express to you how much I hate your guts right now," I told her as Jen entered the room from the hallway, carrying more ice chips, which I had been sucking down all night.

"How's it going?" Jen asked.

"Roughly the same as it was going five minutes ago, Jennifer," I snapped. "In other words, pretty fucking god-awful. Thanks for asking, though."

"Don't call me Jennifer," she said simply as she handed me the ice chips. "Listen, I really think you should reconsider calling Catherine."

"I've told you, I will call Catherine when the baby is here. If I call Catherine right now, the amount of swearing she will hear will cause her to have a stroke. My baby doesn't need that on his conscience."

"Won't she be upset though, when she finds out you had him without telling her?"

"Jen, the conversations I have had with my mother relating to this pregnancy are infuriating and depressing. I would prefer not to discuss her any more tonight, okay? This is supposed to be a joyous night and—fuck!" Another contraction, more pain. God, would this ever end?

Annie came over and squeezed my hand. "It's okay, Gin; it's gonna be okay," she soothed.

"Girls," I gasped, as the pain began to recede, "when it's your turn to do this, screw what anyone says about what's best for the baby. Take the drugs. Believe me, you want the drugs."

* * *

Another three hours, countless more contractions.

I had finally started pushing about an hour ago. I had moved beyond the incessant swearing: I was now too tired to do much talking at all. The girls were amazing, somehow never losing their energy, consistently sitting with me, encouraging me, taking my abuse.

"There's a reason why this is supposed to happen with a person you're married to," I whimpered to Annie once Dr. Beldkin told me he was going to let me have a short break from pushing.

"Why's that, hon?" Annie asked, as she wiped my forehead yet again with a fresh washcloth.

"So at least you're promised to get some from the crazy pregnant lady someday when it's all over," I answered.

"Well I don't usually go that way, but if you're offering..."

I laughed in spite of myself. "God, Annie, what would I do if the two of you weren't here?"

"I don't know. Luckily, none of us will ever find out."

"God, cheese it up much, Ann?"

"Nice," she said, slapping me gently on the shoulder. "Last time I try and tell you how I feel."

"Ginny?" Tammy interrupted. "Ready to push again? We should be getting pretty close now."

I felt like crying. I couldn't believe my break was over already. I was so, so tired—how on earth was I going to be able to do this?

"Ginny?" Jen asked, coming over and grabbing my other hand. "You ready?"

"No!" I cried. I could feel myself panicking and tears started to spill over onto my cheeks. "You guys, I seriously don't think I can do this. Like, for real. It's too hard!" I was really crying now, my breath coming in great hiccupping gasps.

Over the last few months I had become fairly proficient at banishing Josh from my every thought—with a few notable exceptions. But suddenly, there in the delivery room, as I attempted to do the hardest thing I had ever imagined, all I could see was his face in my mind. And I wanted him. I wanted him there with me.

"Ginny," Annie said loudly. "Look at me. Right now."

I did as she asked, gulping and trying to wipe at my eyes.

"You are the strongest person I know—you always have been. You can do this. You can. I know it."

"She's right," Jen said, leaning down to kiss my sweaty, tear-stained cheek. "You can. And when this is over, there's going to be a baby. Our baby, Gin!" Jen was starting to cry now too. "You can do this. And then we'll have our baby boy." She wiped her eyes, then grabbed a tissue and wiped mine too. "So come on," she urged, her voice strong now, unwavering. "Let's go, right now!"

I nodded, and Dr. Beldkin and Tammy moved into position. "Okay, Ginny!" Dr. Beldkin said. "On my count, I want you to push as hard as you can. Ready? Three, two, one, push!"

It was agony. Absolute agony. And terrifying. I felt so weak, and this job felt so, so big. And, worst of all, Josh wasn't there to help me, to pull me through.

But Annie was, and so was Jen, both holding my hands, whispering that they loved me, that they knew I could do it. They were there giving me their strength, and love, as I pushed, and pushed. And they were there when it was finally over, when I could finally rest, there to help me welcome my son into the world.

Chapter Thirty-three

Day One: You did it! You have delivered your healthy, beautiful baby! This is one of the most special times of your life—enjoy it! You may be tempted to keep the baby with you at all times. Let me urge you to take advantage of the hospital's nursery. It's probably the last bit of uninterrupted sleep you'll get for a long time!—Dr. Rebecca Carr, *A Fabulous First Year with Baby!*

I have the cutest baby in the world.

I know that a lot of mothers might say that, they might even believe it, but the truth is, they're all wrong. Because I have the cutest baby in the world.

He was a little bit scary when he first came out. Jen told me it was normal that he was covered in blood and...gunk ("Did you read *any* of the baby books?") but I still felt a lot better after they cleaned him up.

They wrapped him tightly in a blue blanket then put him on my chest. I wasn't sure quite how to hold him—he was so tiny. It looked like he would break if I even touched him. Tammy helped me; she showed me where my arms and hands should go, how I should support his head and keep him upright.

Once he was situated, I stared down into his little face. It was the most surreal thing. He was finally here, after all this time. All of his features were delicate and his skin was so soft. He had a lot of hair for someone who was just born—it looked dark but I couldn't tell yet whether it would have curls. He was so perfect, it took my breath away.

His eyes were huge in his little face, clear and blue and framed by tiny little eyelashes. Tammy told me his eye color could change, but I knew it wouldn't. He had my eyes, just like Josh had pictured.

That was the other thing—he looked like Josh. His little nose and the shape of his chin. It broke my heart a little bit, but it also made me feel strangely proud. He was beautiful.

I would have held him all day if they would have let me. I was completely captivated, and I couldn't imagine anything better than staring at this little face for hours. But eventually they had to take him to get checked over, and I was moving to a smaller room for recovery. Reluctantly I handed him off to Tammy, my eyes following his little rolling bassinet until it was out of sight.

*   *   *

I hated being in the hospital. There were always people coming into my room, poking and prodding me, taking my baby out of my arms and encouraging me to let him go down to the nursery so I could rest better. Yeah right. Like I would be able to rest if he were out of my sight. Besides, Danny slept really well. I started to wonder if all that talk of sleepless nights was an exaggeration. Or maybe my baby was just better than most others.

Annie and Jen were with us as much as possible. I knew they were exhausted, but I think they were (nearly) as in love with Danny as I was. I convinced them to go home and sleep for a while the night after he was born. They came back in the morning with flowers, balloons, and treats for me. They did better than any daddy ever could.

A lactation specialist came in to show me how to nurse. It was very weird and I had a hard time getting used to it. Annie declared it "icky", and I kind of agreed with her, though I would never admit it. It was supposed to be better for the baby, though, so I decided to stick with it.

The morning after Danny was born, a doctor came by to talk to me about circumcision. I was very torn, and I wished there was a man in my life whose advice I could ask. I hated the idea of them hurting my baby, for any reason. However...

"Have either of you ever been with an uncircumcised guy?" I asked Annie and Jen, after the doctor had left us alone.

"Nope, never," Annie said.

"I have," Jen shrugged. "It wasn't a big deal."

"Are you sure?" I demanded. "I don't want him to have problems later with girls. I don't want him to feel different or anything."

"It really wasn't a big deal for me," Jen assured me. "It definitely wouldn't keep me from a good guy. I don't think you need to worry."

If Danny could someday end up with a girl as amazing as Jen, I decided it didn't matter. I declined the circumcision—and immediately felt relieved.

My parents came to visit on the second day. They both managed to behave themselves, though my dad was clearly uncomfortable. It pissed me off that he wasn't effusively in love with Danny, but I tried to keep a lid on it. My mother held him, declared him a beautiful baby, and they were off. I knew my poor mothering skills would open up a whole new realm of criticism for her, but I figured it would at least keep us talking.

*   *   *

Danny was born early on Saturday morning. They let me go home with him on Monday. Annie and Jen had both taken the morning off so they could be with me. We spent about half an hour picking out the perfect outfit for him. Annie had brought several of the things we got at the shower back to the hospital for me to choose from—but they had both gone out and purchased a few more outfits. With the three of us around, this boy would never want for fashion.

Finally we decided on a green romper decorated with little monkeys. It was adorable, and he totally rocked it out, if I do say so myself.

After the nurse came out to inspect that our car seat was properly installed, we were off. I sat in the back with Danny. Every bump and turn Jen made would send me into panic. I could imagine a million terrible scenarios in which something happened to my baby—and we hadn't even gotten home yet.

217

We pulled up in the driveway and I promptly burst into tears. The girls had decorated the entire yard and front porch. There were streamers and balloons everywhere and a giant cardboard stork bearing a sign which read, "Welcome Home, Baby Danny and Mommy Ginny!" It was so nice of them.

"God, you cry an awful lot these days," Annie muttered as she got out of the car. "It's like you're turning into one of *those girls* in front of my eyes."

I got out of the car as well and walked around to Danny's side to unstrap him from his seat. He was wide awake and blinking up at me. "Danny," I said to him happily, "this is your home, baby."

"Yeah, it's a chick's pad, buddy, so you better just deal with it," Annie told him in mock-serious tones.

I walked him into the house, looking around happily. I loved this place, and now my baby was here. "Things are gonna be great," I whispered to him. "Just you wait and see."

Chapter Thirty-four

I thought being pregnant was hard. And labor was pretty awful. But they had nothing, *nothing,* on having a newborn in the house.

I was exhausted. Every time I would close my eyes Danny would wake up screaming. It was almost like he was doing it on purpose. My perfect little sweet baby from the hospital had turned into a screaming, demanding terror—impossible to keep satisfied. "Just like a man," Annie sneered in exhaustion.

The girls helped out as best they could, but knowing they both had work, I just couldn't let them stay up with me at night—though they offered. I'm sure the screaming kept them awake plenty. When they would get home they would demand I go to bed for a few hours while they dealt with Danny. Those were the only hours of sleep I got for the first two weeks.

My nipples were sore. They don't tell you much about that when extolling the amazingness of childbirth. And I was constipated. And I had hemorrhoids. Sexy stuff here, folks. It was a good thing I was man-less, to be honest. Who would ever want to sleep with me again?

There were moments, perfect moments, that made up for all the awfulness, more or less. The first time Danny clutched my finger was pretty amazing—how could he be so strong? Giving him a bath was awesome, too. I would set his little plastic tub up on our kitchen table and lay him in the warm water, inspecting every inch of his little baby body. I would gently splash water on his tummy to make his eyes go big with surprise. And then I would dry him off, cover him with lotion, and snuggle him until he was warm again.

Every time Danny made eye contact with me, it would pretty much take my breath away. He could stare at me for so long, with such intensity. I couldn't remember anyone else ever looking at me like that.

Because of that, even the breast feeding lost its weirdness with time. When Danny was eating he would stare up at me, unblinking, like he was memorizing my face. I started to really enjoy those moments when it was just him and me, holding him so close, feeling the way his body would move against me with each tiny breath.

His diapers were a different story. How could such a tiny person create such a mess? I was, for the first time, grateful that I had spent so much time babysitting. Changing dirty diapers rarely fazed me anymore. Besides which, I was usually too exhausted to take too much notice of anything, horrible diaper fragrances included.

Jen, on the other hand, seemed to have plenty of energy to notice everything. Every day when she would get home from work she would sweep Danny up into her arms, kissing his face and cooing at him. It was pretty sweet—until the questions started. "How much did he eat today? Did he poo? What did it look like?" She was driving me slightly crazy—but as the interrogation was generally followed by her insisting I go to bed for a while, I never complained.

Annie was the complete opposite. She could care less about issues relating to his eating, digestion, or sleeping habits. Annie treated him, not like a baby, but like she would any other member of the household. She would take him from my arms and walk away with him, talking to him in a low serious voice more often used when talking to grown-ups. Walking him to her bedroom, she would show him the contents of her wardrobe, explaining the differences between the various fabrics. Or read aloud to him from Rolling Stone magazine, explaining which bands were good and which bands were crap.

One Saturday, when Danny was about three weeks old, Annie offered to watch him for a bit so I could get some stuff done around the house. I knew she had a really big audition that coming week, so I was touched that she would take time out of rehearsing to help.

As I was heading to the laundry room with yet another load of Danny's dirty clothes and burp rags, I happened by her room—where she was performing an unfamiliar monologue—one that was clearly peppered with swear words and appeared to be about prostitution. I was worried for a moment: surely this was too mature for a newborn. But then I looked at

Danny, sitting calmly in his chair. He was staring at her, wide-eyed, and seemed perfectly content and calm. I realized that he was simply enthralled by her voice, her energy, regardless of what she was saying. Smiling, I continued on with the laundry.

As I put his folded things back in his drawers, I heard Annie moving around downstairs, talking to him softly. "You would just have to blow out your diaper as soon as Annie took over, wouldn't you? You couldn't save it for Mommy or for Aunt Jen, could you?...Oh God, kid, seriously? How is that even possible?" I heard Annie making exaggerated gagging noises and I couldn't help but laugh—but I was in no hurry to go help.

After a few moments of silence, I heard something that made my blood run cold: Annie yelped.

I bolted down the stairs as fast as I could. She was shouting for me now, and she sounded really freaked out. I reached the living room with Jen hot on my heels. Annie was kneeling in front of Danny, who was laying on his changing mat on the floor. At first, I couldn't tell what was wrong. I could see that his chest was moving and there was no blood...

"What, what is it?" I gasped.

"Something fell off of him!" she cried. "I don't know what it is! I was just putting his diaper back on and..."

"You dope," Jen said, kneeling next to her. "That's just his umbilical cord."

"Is it supposed to fall off?" I asked, still inwardly panicking.

"*Yes,*" Jen exclaimed, clearly exasperated. "Seriously, Ginny, how have you not read the baby book?"

"I have!" I said. "Well, I mean, I've read a lot of it. I tend to gravitate towards chapters about signs to look for that he might be sick or something. That's kind of my main worry."

She laughed at me. "Gin, your baby is fine. Nothing is going to hurt him. Maybe you need to bone up on the day to day stuff instead."

"Here's a bigger problem," Annie said. "What the heck are we supposed to *do* with that thing?"

"I guess you just throw it away," Jen said, shrugging.

"I'm not picking it up!" Annie insisted.

I looked at Jen, but for all her expertise, she was determinedly not meeting my eyes.

"Fine," I sighed, picking up a tissue to wrap the umbilical cord in. As I picked it up, I glared at the girls. "I cannot wait until it's your turn for all of this!"

Chapter Thirty-five

One month: This is a great time for Baby to start practicing his Tummy Time—a very important part of your baby's development that will help him with his motor skills. Hearing you speak is also very important to your baby's development. While you're down there on your tummies, it's a great time to talk to Baby—and with his coos and gurgles he might just talk back! It is very common for moms to be feeling very hormonal four weeks in. Try to take good care of yourself and make sure you have someone to talk to about your feelings. Hand Baby over to Dad and get out for some you-time. You deserve it!—Dr. Rebecca Carr, A Fabulous First Year with Baby!

When Jen came home from work on Thursday afternoon, I was sprawled out on the living room floor, Danny lying on a quilt next to me. We were both crying hysterically.

"Ginny?" she shouted over the noise. "What's going on? Is something wrong?"

I only cried harder.

Jen knelt down next to me and picked up Danny, bouncing him gently in one arm while she rubbed my back with her other hand. "It's okay, sweetie," she soothed. "Everything's fine."

I wasn't sure which of us she was trying to comfort.

Eventually Danny stopped crying in her arms. I lay there for a long time, letting her rub my back, before I finally took a deep breath and sat up.

"There," she said quietly. "That's better." She reached over to Danny's basket and pulled out a burp rag, holding it out to me so I could wipe my face. "You wanna talk about it?"

I took a shuddering breath. "It's stupid," I gulped.

Jen smiled at me. "Doesn't matter. I still want to hear."

"The book says we're supposed to be doing tummy time," I started in a rush. "So I've been trying to get him to lay on his belly with me, but every time I did, he started wailing! And today, all I could think was that if he doesn't practice his tummy time, he's never going to have a strong neck. And if his neck doesn't get strong, he won't be able to sit up. And if he can't sit up, he'll never crawl..." I was crying again, taking big shuddering gasps as tears spilled down my checks.

"Ginny," she said calmly. "You're spiraling. So he didn't feel like being on his tummy today. Maybe he has gas. Maybe he's full. Maybe he wanted to be held. It's okay, I promise."

"You don't think it means something's wrong?" I gulped.

"Nope," she said. "I think he's perfect." He did look pretty perfect now, sleeping in her arms. "You know what else I think?" she continued. "I think you need to get out of this house for a little while."

"I do get out of the house," I argued. "I take Danny for a walk every day. And we sit out on the porch when it's not too hot."

"I mean *without* Danny," she replied. "You need to get out of this house and have some time to yourself."

I stared at her in bewilderment. Without Danny? Was she insane?

"Are you insane?" I asked.

"No," she said. "I am very wise. You need a break."

"I'm not leaving Danny here," I said. "No way."

"Ginny, I watch him all the time. I know what I'm doing. He'll be fine. Besides, in a couple weeks you're going to be heading back to work." I felt a sharp stab in my stomach at the thought. "I think it would be good for you to start getting some practice now."

I couldn't deny she had a point. But the thought of leaving him...

"What would I even do?" I asked her. I was having a hard time picturing the world outside my baby. What did I do in my free time before he came along?

"You could go get a mani-pedi," she suggested. "That would probably relax you."

Oh. A mani-pedi. A beauty salon. I loved stuff like that, getting pampered. And it had been so, so long...

"I'm gonna bet by the glazed look in your eyes that a mani-pedi sounds good to you," she laughed. "You should go. Annie will be home any minute to give me a hand. It'll take you, like, an hour. And then you'll be back with Danny."

It was tempting, I had to admit. So very tempting.
"Ginny, just go."

* * *

Ten minutes later I was in my car, heading into
Royal Oak and my favorite salon. I couldn't help but
feel excited. I had always loved beauty salons, even
when I was little and would have to sit and wait while
my mom had her hair set. There was something about
the smell, the buzz of female conversation, the air of
expectation and excitement. A day at the salon could
always boost my spirits.

The technician set me up in a comfortable chair
and eased my feet into the spa bath. I almost moaned
at the contact—the warm water and the bubbles felt
amazing. I hadn't realized how much my feet ached, or
how sore my back was. I looked around the arms of the
chair and found, to my excitement, a control panel.
These chairs were massaging. Ahhh.

I let the sounds of talk and laughter, the warm
water, and the pressure on my back wash over me,
until my worries about leaving Danny faded to a low
buzz in the back of my mind. For the first time in
weeks, I was starting to feel like myself.

* * *

"Something happened," Annie said, meeting me at
the door. I felt my heart stop. Danny.

"What?" I asked, grabbing her arm. "Where is he?
What's wrong?"

"The baby's fine!" Jen called out from inside.

"Oh God, yeah, sorry," Annie said hurriedly, pulling me into the house. "Sorry. Danny's totally okay."

I could have slapped her. I tried to catch my breath. "You *scared* me!" I said.

"Sorry, sorry!" she said again. I pushed her aside and walked upstairs to my bedroom. Regardless of her assurances, I wasn't going to feel completely better until I actually held my baby. He was awake in his crib, cooing and staring at his fingers as I peered over the bars. "Hiya, little man!" I said, reaching down to pick him up.

"Ginny, wait a second," Annie said, grabbing my arm. "I have to tell you something, and I'm not sure you should be holding Danny when I do it."

I stared at her. "What's going on, Ann?" I demanded.

She bit her lip. "Maybe you should sit down," she said.

"Oh for God's sake, Annie, just tell me what the hell is going on!"

"Josh came here."

I froze. Josh? He was here? In the house with Danny? Feeling a panic I could not explain, I reached down and plucked him up from his crib, holding him close to me. "What did he want?" I whispered.

"I have no idea," she replied. "I didn't let him say much." She looked slightly sheepish. "I swore quite a bit, to be honest. I told him he was an asshole—well, I called him worse than that, actually. Anyways, I told him to get the hell out of here and not to come back."

"Did he see the baby?" I asked.

"No!" she said vehemently. "I never would have let him! I didn't even give him the chance to ask, I had his ass off that porch so quick!"

"I was up here with Danny," Jen assured me. "He never saw us."

I felt a surge of affection for them. I should have known they'd protect Danny.

"Why was he here?" I asked. "What could he have wanted? You don't think..." I looked at the girls in panic. "You don't think he changed his mind, do you? You don't think he would try to get Danny away from me?" The thought made my heart race all over again.

"Ginny," Jen said firmly. "Don't jump to conclusions. You have no idea what he wanted. Maybe he's just feeling guilty. Maybe he just wanted to see him. Try not to worry."

I hugged my baby tighter to me, breathing in the scent of his sweet little head, trying to calm myself down.

"Ginny, he asked me to tell you he'd stop by again," Annie said. "I told him he better not, but...maybe you should be prepared to see him."

"Did you tell him where I was?" I asked. "Do you think he'd come back tonight?"

"I doubt it," Annie said sheepishly. "I told him you were at work...I kinda played you up a little bit, to be honest."

"What do you mean?"

"She went on and on about how great you're doing," Jen said, rolling her eyes. "I could hear her from upstairs. Telling him you didn't need him, that you had an awesome job running a bookstore, and how super busy and important you are these days."

"You told Josh all that about me?" I asked Annie. She shrugged. I could have kissed her.

Chapter Thirty-six

I tried to keep Josh out of my head that night, but it was next to impossible. I stayed busy, kept my thoughts occupied, but every so often I would feel a flash of panic. What if he wanted my baby? I painted elaborate what-if scenarios in my head, involving his parents conspiring with lawyers and police and other shadowy figures to somehow get to Danny. I knew it was ridiculous and unlikely, but I couldn't shake the fear.

I slept badly. I dreamt of Mrs. Stanley, of waking up to find Danny's crib empty. My clock said it was three a.m. when I finally got up and pulled him into bed with me. I put pillows around his tiny body to prevent any rolling, and then lay awake staring at him. I felt calmer with him near me, but sleep continued to elude me.

It was strange: a year or so ago I would have listed Josh as the most important thing in my life. In such a short amount of time, Danny had completely eclipsed him, eclipsed everything in my life. I never understood it when people talked about their kids being their whole life. I assumed they were exaggerating, or saying what they thought was the PC sentiment. I didn't understand it.

I got it now. I didn't know why Josh was in town, or what he wanted, but I knew I would do anything, absolutely anything, to keep Danny safe and with me.

*   *   *

Danny was an angel the next morning. He slept for four hours after his six a.m. feeding. By then I was so exhausted from my night of worry that I fell asleep instantly. I woke up to him gurgling in his crib, and felt more refreshed than was generally normal for me these days.

I was getting into a routine with my little man, carrying him around the house with me as I went about my day. After I ate some breakfast— one-handed at the kitchen counter so I could cradle him with my other arm—I strapped Danny into his bouncy seat and brought him into the bathroom with me so I could shower. While I shampooed my hair I could hear him cooing and gurgling. He had recently discovered his hands, and looking at them could provide hours of entertainment.

I threw on an old sundress and put my hair up in a messy ponytail (I never had time for my blow dryer these days) then brought Danny downstairs for his tummy time. Jen had been right: he did much better today. After doing some laundry, I took Danny outside to his stroller. I strapped him in and set off around the neighborhood. I was a beautiful day: sunny and warm but not overwhelming. We were fast approaching September and the autumn, which meant I would be going back to work soon. Every time I thought of it I got a knot in my stomach, so I avoided the subject as much as I could.

Danny fell asleep on our walk. When we got back to the house I lifted him as gently as possible and laid him in his crib—he didn't stir one bit. I stared down at him as he slept and resisted the urge to brush his cheek. As he had gotten older his cheeks had filled out some, as had his chubby arms and legs. He was now squishy and soft and so perfect. I breathed in that baby smell one more time, then crept from the room.

Just as I eased the door shut behind me, the doorbell rang. I cursed and froze, listening hard through the door to hear if Danny had woken up. I couldn't hear a sound, so I headed downstairs to see who was at the door.

I should have known. I mean, I had been worrying about it all night. But the morning had been a good one, and it had allowed me to fall into a false sense of security. What a mistake.

It was Josh.

*   *   *

I didn't know what to say to him. When I looked at his face, all I could see was Danny. So many of their features were the same. Thinking of Danny, and of Josh not wanting him, filled me with rage. I had to work to keep my hands from trembling, to keep myself from lunging at him, striking him...

He just stood in the doorway, looking at me. Neither of us said a word. Finally, I moved aside and motioned for him to come in. As he crossed the threshold, I stepped as far away from him as I could in the small foyer. I didn't want him to touch me, not even by accident.

He walked awkwardly into the living room and sat on the couch. I saw his eyes flicker across Danny's bouncy seat, but he didn't mention it. I stayed where I was, half in the foyer and half in the living room, staring at him. It was so surreal to see him here, after all this time.

He cleared his throat, his eyes on his feet. After what felt like a lifetime he looked up at me. "Hey, Gin."

I still couldn't find my voice so I merely nodded at him. He appeared to flinch slightly at my reaction, but he covered it quickly.

"I know this is awful," he said. "Me coming here like this, barging in on you. I hope it's not too much trouble."

"It's fine," I said at last. "What, uh, what can I do for you?"

He smiled slightly. "It's good to see you, Ginny. You look good."

"Do I?" I asked in surprise. I wondered what he saw when he looked at me. Would I look different to him? I *felt* like such a different person from the last time I had seen him.

"Yeah." He was smiling for real now. "You look...happy."

Hmm. "Well," I said slowly. "I guess that's because I am."

"Annie said you had a new job?" he asked politely. "You run a bookstore?"

"Yeah," I replied, determined to give him as little detail about our lives as I could.

He looked awkward again. "You're pretty pissed at me, aren't you?" he asked.

I couldn't believe he would even ask me such a thing. I wanted to scream at him, to throw him out of my house, to swear he would have nothing to do with me and Danny ever again.

I took a deep, steadying breath. "I'm fine," I said shortly.

"Look, I'm sorry about everything," he said, his voice dropping with intensity. "I swear to God, Ginny, I'm so sorry. I thought it would be better for you if I just disappeared, if you never had to think about me again."

"You thought that would be better for us?" I asked coldly. "Great. So why'd you change your mind?"

"Because I miss you."

I was still standing across the room from him, but instinctively I took a step back. He couldn't be doing this. He couldn't actually be here to tell me that he missed me. A million questions raced through my mind and I threw out the first one I could grasp.

"What about Amy?" My voice surprised me—it sounded like it was laced with acid.

"Amy?" he asked, confusion on his face. "What about her?"

I laughed and my laugh was bitter. I hated that he was bringing these things out of me, that he was polluting Danny's house with this anger and poison. "I get it. You miss me, but not in a way that would upset her."

"Ginny, what are you talking about?"

I paused. Josh was not one to play dumb. Was I missing something?

"Amy. Your fiancé."

He stared at me, his mouth open with shock. "My what?"

I started to feel some emotion welling up inside me, but I couldn't name it. Confusion? Fear?

"Amy, Josh." I said each word distinctly so there would be no mistake. "Amy Harper from *StateInk*. Your *fiancé.*"

He was silent for several moments. I realized that my knees were shaking and thought absently that I should sit down.

"Where they hell did you get that from?" he finally said, his voice heavy with confusion.

I stared at him. Was this a joke?

"From your mother," I said uncertainly. "When I saw her that day at the coffee house, she told me. She had a picture of the two of you. She said you were going to Seattle together and you were getting married—"

"Ginny," he cut me off, standing up and taking a step towards me. "I have no idea what you're talking about. You saw my mother?"

Wait. Wait a second. He had to know that I had seen his mother. He had to know because that's how he knew about Danny. I felt the world start to spin.

"Josh?" I said, uncertainly, wanting to ask what was going on, wanting to make sense of this insanity.

"Listen," he said clearly, taking another step towards me. "I don't know what's going on here, but I swear to you, I didn't go to Seattle with Amy, or anyone else. Ginny, I'm not engaged."

I realized belatedly that I should have sat when I had the chance. Now it was too late, and the floor was rushing up to meet me.

Chapter Thirty-seven

"Ginny."

I knew that voice.

"Ginny, wake up."

I had a crazy idea that it was Danny, but that didn't make sense. He was a baby. How would he have gotten down the stairs? And when would he have learned how to talk?

I opened my eyes and saw Josh looking down at me. For one second, as my eyes met his, I felt like it had all gone back to normal, the way it was supposed to be. I was in Josh's arms and he was looking at me like he might just love me.

But that couldn't be true either. I blinked again and tried to sit up.

"Be careful!" he urged, and I moved more cautiously.

"What happened?" I asked, rubbing my eyes.

"You fainted." Josh looked very worried. "How do you feel? Can I get you some water?"

He was sitting far too close to me. I couldn't deal with him sitting that close to me, looking at me with so much concern. I shook my head and moved quickly to the other end of the couch. "I'm okay."

"Let me get you some water," Josh insisted, standing up and heading into the kitchen. I didn't like the idea of him in there, where I couldn't see him, moving confidently around my house like he was comfortable here.

He was back quickly, holding out a glass of water to me. When I took it, he sat down, much closer to my end of the couch than I was comfortable with. I took a deep breath and drank the water, trying to clear my head.

What was going on here? What had he said that had made everything go all swirly and fuzzy like that?

Amy. Oh yeah. He had told me he wasn't engaged to Amy.

But there was something else, too. Something else that mattered, that changed things...but I couldn't think of it.

"Is that better?" he asked after a minute. "How do you feel?"

"I'm fine. I don't know what happened there. I'm sorry."

"Don't apologize!" He looked really shaken up though, like he too couldn't figure out what was going on.

"Josh." I paused, trying to figure out the right questions to ask. Everything felt so muddled. "What's going on? Your mom told me—"

"I don't understand," he interrupted. "You saw my mom? When? Why?"

Was it possible he was joking? Or trying to pretend that he hadn't acted so horribly, abandoning me and the baby the way he had?

I looked at him levelly. "Josh, I saw your mother because you refused to meet me. So she came instead. She gave me the letter—the letter *you* wrote me."

He merely shook his head. "Ginny, I never wrote you a letter—well, that's not really true. I wrote you one every other day, trying to explain. But I never sent you one, and I certainly never gave one to my mom for you."

"But I read it," I insisted. "It was your handwriting, Josh—" But that wasn't quite true either. I saw the envelope, which did look like his handwriting. But I never actually read the letter, not personally. I had let Annie read it...

"Hang on," I said, standing up. "Stay right there!" I ran up the stairs, trying to be quiet. The last thing in the world I needed right now was for Danny to wake up. I tiptoed into the bedroom, opened the bottom drawer of my desk, and crept back out again. I made it downstairs without hearing a noise from the baby, and I thanked the Lord for small favors.

I sat next to Josh on the couch and pulled the letter from the envelope. There were his words, those horrible words that had changed everything. But there was something wrong. It looked like his handwriting, almost exactly...but it wasn't.

"What is that, Ginny?" he demanded, his voice shaking. Unable to answer, I handed it to him. Possibilities were washing over me and I didn't know what to believe, couldn't understand what had happened, what *was* happening.

"What the hell..." he muttered, reading through the letter. "My *mother* gave this to you? I didn't write this!" He looked up at me, his eyes confused, anger and fear creeping into his voice.

"I never read it," I whispered. "Annie read it to me. I just assumed it was you, because she said..."

But he wasn't listening to me. He had returned to the letter and was rereading it slowly, his mouth forming the words as if trying to force them to make sense. "What is this part, about the money?" he asked, looking up. "Why would my parents give you money?"

I couldn't speak. If he didn't write this, if he didn't know that I was meeting his mother...could that mean...could it be possible that he *didn't know*? About *any* of it?

He was scared now, really scared. I could tell. He reached out and grabbed my arm, his grip tight, almost painful. "Ginny, you have to tell me what the hell is going on. Please."

Then my luck ran out. Above us, Danny woke up, and our baby started to cry.

Chapter Thirty-eight

Josh froze, his fingers digging into my arm. Danny's cries grew louder—he was not accustomed to waiting for me, the spoiled little angel. I closed my eyes. Oh my God.

"Ginny," Josh's voice was hoarse. "What...what is that?"

"You need to leave, Josh."

"What? Are you kidding me? I'm not going anywhere!" He was shouting now, the noise and the crying of the baby surrounding me, invading my mind, making it impossible to think.

"Please, just go," I begged, and tears were slipping from my eyes, blurring his face, making everything that much more confusing.

"Who's crying?" he demanded. "What is that?"

I wrenched my arm away from him. I had to get to Danny. He needed me. Maybe everything would make sense once I was holding my baby. I stood shakily, walking toward the stairs. "Stay here," I begged. "Please."

It was no good: Josh was right behind me, following me into my room, where the baby's cries were reaching the upper decibels. I tried to ignore Josh, tried to pretend this wasn't happening, so that I could focus on Danny. I picked him up from his crib, holding him close to me, soothing him, but his cries did not abate.

"Oh my God."

I tried to tune Josh out. Danny was crying, I was crying, and I just wanted to go back to this morning, before any of this had happened.

"Is that your baby?" Josh shouted behind me.

"It's okay, Danny," I whispered. "It's okay, sweet boy, Mama's here."

"What the hell is going on?" It was Annie. Sometime in the middle of all of this she had arrived home and was now standing in my doorway, mouth open in surprise.

"That's what I want to know!" Josh shouted. "Who *is* that?" He pointed his finger at me, but I knew he was really pointing at Danny, and something about it broke my heart.

"That's your baby, you asshole," Annie snarled. "Now get the hell out of our house."

* * *

I don't know what would have happened if Jen hadn't come home then. She heard the shouting, came up to my room, and took in the scene before her. I couldn't imagine what she was thinking, seeing the four of us like this—Josh, here in our house, Annie, ready to pounce on him, Danny screaming, and me holding the baby like my life depended on it while I sobbed.

She immediately walked over to me and held out her arms. "Give me Danny," she said calmly. I only held him to me tighter. "It's okay, Gin. Give me Danny." Reluctantly, I handed him over.

Without him to hold onto, I felt bereft. How was I going to handle this?

"Now everyone shut up," she demanded. "Or go downstairs." She began walking Danny around the room, talking to him softly, patting his back. Josh and I watched her, as if mesmerized, as she calmed the baby—Annie, on the other hand, continued to stare daggers at Josh.

When Danny had finally calmed down, Jen eased him back into his crib and pointed at the stairs. The three of us followed her in silence. I wasn't sure, but I think Josh was in shock—hell, I think I was in shock too.

"Okay," Annie said, once we were downstairs. "What the fuck is going on?"

I looked at Josh. He appeared completely shell-shocked, his face a grayish color, his hands clearly trembling. Something about seeing him that way calmed me down. "It would appear that Josh didn't know about the baby," I replied.

Jen looked at me sharply, but Annie merely snorted. "Yeah, sure."

Josh didn't respond. He was staring at the bouncy chair, the same one he had seen but overlooked when he arrived.

Annie was staring at me. "You don't actually believe this, do you?" she demanded. "After everything he's done to you?" When I didn't reply she grabbed my arm. "We read the letter, Ginny!"

"He didn't write it."

She stared at me like I was mad.

"Really, Ann, it wasn't his handwriting. The writing on the envelope looked like his, but I never saw the letter itself. If I would have…"

"It's my dad's," Josh said quietly. "My dad's handwriting. It's pretty similar, but it wasn't me."

I closed my eyes. What could have been avoided if I would have just read the letter myself, if I hadn't been so chicken.

"What would you have done differently?" Annie demanded, as if reading my thoughts. "He changed his fucking number, remember? And didn't tell you his address. And," she was practically hissing with anger now, "he sent his *mother* to tell you that he wanted nothing to do with you and your baby."

"Annie, I think we should go," Jen said quietly. She was looking at Josh, who appeared close to passing out himself. "We should let them talk."

"I'm not leaving her alone with him," Annie said flatly. "No way."

"Come on," Jen insisted. "We'll just take a walk; we won't go far." Annie looked at me, as if asking what she should do. I nodded at her, and she blew out a gust of air.

"Fine. But I swear to God, Josh, if you do anything to fuck with her, I will rip your balls off." She walked ahead of Jen and slammed out of the house.

Jen took my hand. "Are you okay?" I nodded at her. She squeezed my hand and followed Annie.

I turned to Josh. "Well," I sighed. "I guess we'd better talk."

*   *   *

It took a while to explain things. Josh seemed to be having trouble comprehending what I was telling him, and he deviated between anger, shock, and disbelief.

"Why didn't you try to find me?" he demanded, when I told him how his mother had met me at the coffee house.

"She told me you were in Seattle, and she wouldn't give me your number."

"But how could you have thought I would do that to you?"

"I didn't," I whispered. "I argued with her, demanded that she let me talk to you. But she refused. She said you didn't want anything to do with me. And then she gave me the letter, and showed me the picture of you and Amy."

"I didn't give her a picture of me and Amy. Why would I?" he demanded.

"She had one, Josh."

He was quiet for a moment. "I just don't get why she would do this."

"She never liked me; you know that."

"But to keep me from my... son? How could she do that to me? How could *you* do that to me?"

Okay, I'd had about enough of that. I got that he was upset, but there was no reason whatsoever for him to blame me. "Of the two of us, *Josh*, you are the only one who had the other's phone number," I reminded him.

"I'm sorry." He seemed to deflate in front of me. "That's why I came, to tell you how sorry I was for never calling."

"Why didn't you call?" I whispered, feeling the hurt of it deeply. I could understand, maybe even accept, that everything with the baby had been a huge misunderstanding. But he had never called, in all these months.

"You asked me not to," he reminded me.

"I asked you not to call for *a while*," I told him. "It's been ten months, Josh."

He sighed. "I know. I'm sorry."

"You've been saying that an awful lot today," I muttered.

"Ginny, I thought about you every day. Every single day. I wrote you over a hundred letters. When I was in Seattle, I saw your face on every girl I met. I haven't been able to get you out of my mind. When I said I came back because I missed you, I meant it."

I was speechless. What was he trying to tell me?

"Look, I get that that stuff isn't what's important right now," he sighed. "But I wanted you to know. I didn't go off and forget about you, Ginny. But I was afraid if I called you, or tried to see you, I wouldn't be able to stop myself and we'd be right back where we were last June."

I nodded, knowing he was right. Of course we would have reverted to our old patterns.

"I can't imagine you doing all of this alone," he whispered, tears filling his eyes. "Thinking I didn't want to be here."

"I wasn't alone," I told him. "Annie and Jen were amazing."

"Were you scared?"

"Terrified."

Josh was really crying now. "You don't have to tell me, Ginny, I know you probably hate me, but...what's he like? The baby?"

I was so glad he asked. I had been terrified that he didn't care, that he really didn't want to know Danny, even now that he knew about him.

"He's amazing," I said. "Absolutely amazing." I looked over at Josh. He was watching me, enthralled. "He cries a lot, I think mostly to piss me off when I'm tired." I laughed a little. "But as soon as he looks at me, I forgive him. He looks like you."

We were both quiet for a moment.

"You're different, Gin," he finally said. "Something about you is different."

I shrugged. "It's been quite a year."

Josh looked sad again. "And you had to do it on your own," he murmured. "I'm so, so sorry."

I couldn't answer him. I felt sad then too, thinking of how different it all could have been. For me, and for Danny.

"I need to go," Josh said suddenly, startling me. "I need to go see my parents. I can't believe they would do this to me. I literally cannot believe it."

"I take it they didn't know you were coming here?"

He snorted. "No. I wonder what they would have done to keep me away." He laughed bitterly. "Did they honestly think I would never see you again? How stupid could they be?" He clenched his fists, and it occurred to me that he was absolutely furious. I stood up, ready to walk him to the door, but he hesitated. "Do you think...I mean, would you mind, if I see him? Just real quick, before I go?" I gave him a slight smile. "Sure." I led Josh back up the stairs to my room. Peering into the crib, I saw that Danny had woken up. He wasn't crying or fussing, just gurgling softly to himself. "He's discovered his hands," I explained. "He thinks they're the most fascinating creation in history."

I leaned down and picked him up, nuzzling his face before turning him so Josh could see him. He stared at his son, and I felt a lump rise in my throat. "He's amazing."

"He's perfect," I corrected. "The most perfect thing in the world."

"And you named him...Danny?" He met my gaze and I knew in that moment that he remembered, too. The lump in my throat swelled and I could only nod in response.

Josh reached out his hand, as if he wanted to touch Danny.

"It's okay," I told him. "You can touch him."

Josh moved closer, and Danny seized his finger, wrapping his whole hand around it and squeezing.

"He's pretty strong," I laughed.

Josh just stared at him. I had thought I knew all of his expressions, all of his smiles. But this one was foreign to me. This one was just for Danny.

Chapter Thirty-nine

Two months: Can you believe the changes in your baby since you first brought him home from the hospital? Chances are, by this time your baby is able to gurgle and coo, grab your fingers (isn't he strong?), hold his head up, smile at you (so precious!), and, most importantly, sleep for stretches of several hours at a time. What a relief! If you are getting ready to head back to work, it's important that you find child care that you are comfortable with. Try not to feel guilty about leaving—your baby can handle it!—Dr. Rebecca Carr, *A Fabulous First Year with Baby!*

I am a terrible mother. A terrible person, really.

This is how I felt pretty much every morning though, so I guess I should just try to get used to it.

Going back to work was *hard*. Like, really, really hard. I hated leaving Danny. I hated being away from him, I hated thinking about someone else taking care of him.

Usually, by the time I drove to Rochester and actually started working, I felt better. I still loved my job. Just Books had grown to be one of my favorite

251

places in the world, and managing was so much more fun than being a clerk.

The Wrights continued to be amazing employers. They allowed me one shift a week to work purely on managerial duties—meaning I could be locked up in the office all day, not having to deal with customers. The best part about that arrangement is I could have Danny with me at the store once a week. When he got bigger, we would probably have to re-think it, but for now he seemed generally content to spend an afternoon in his bouncy chair while I worked. Okay, to be perfectly honest, most of the time he insisted I hold him, or at least keep him strapped to my chest in the Baby Bjorn, but I was getting really good at working one-handed.

Mr. Wright had loved being back at the store during my maternity leave. He had loved it so much that his doctor (and his wife), had agreed that he should be allowed to spend a few hours each day there. With some creative scheduling on my part, and *a lot* of help from the girls, I was able to spend as much time as possible with Danny and only had to leave him with a stranger for a dozen or so hours a week. This made me feel better, less guilty—and it also saved me a ton of money.

My hours at the store passed pretty quickly that day. I had Beth in helping me and we were pretty busy, which always made the time go by faster. I had recently set up a promotion to celebrate the back to school season: if people brought in a used book to donate to a school, they received a buy-one-get-one-free coupon to use in our store. The boxes of donated books, and the noticeable up-tick in our sales, was making me feel pretty good.

I was eager to get home at the end of the shift. Annie and I usually had a fight about who got to give the baby a bath—rarely was Danny more sweet, or more happy, than he was at bath time. He would usually be awake for a few more hours, alert and playful until it was time for his last feeding, when I could rock him to my heart's content.

After he was down for the night—or, at least, down until his three a.m. feeding—Josh would usually call to check in.

After Josh had found out about the baby, he called work and requested some vacation time, allowing him to stay for a week. He holed up in a hotel—he wasn't speaking to his parents at all—but spent most of his waking hours at the house with Danny.

It was clear he was madly in love with the baby, and Danny seemed absolutely enthralled by him. Annie put it down to the fact that he had never been exposed to any testosterone in his life, but I had a feeling Danny felt bonded to his father.

It was hard for me, having Josh in the house like that. And though I was so happy for Danny that his dad cared about him, it was hard for me to see Josh with the baby. I had dreamt of Josh and I having a family together so many times, for so long. I had to work very hard to not pretend that we were together again. I was liable to take his affection for Danny, and his kindness to me, and turn it into a fantasy that he loved me and we were still together. Those thoughts were dangerous, so I tried to keep them turned off.

For my part, I still loved Josh.

I had discovered this very early on; probably the second day that he was home. He was just pulling on his sweatshirt, getting ready to leave for the evening, and I felt a tug. I didn't want him to go. I wanted him to be there with me, and with Danny, all night— always. I still loved him.

I was pretty mad at myself for this realization, obviously. I had worked so hard on my independence, worked so hard to get over Josh, and for what? Even after everything that had happened I was still madly and hopelessly in love with him. What was wrong with me?

Jen knew at once, of course. She had accepted the tentative situation of Josh being around with fairly good grace. Annie had a much harder time with it. Her anger with him had not abated and she had a hard time even being in the same room with him.

One night, after Josh had left and Danny had been put to bed, Jen and I took some iced tea to the front porch. The summer was still hanging on but autumn was fast approaching, and we wanted to enjoy the warm night while we still had the chance. It was gorgeous outside, still and clear, and we sat in comfortable silence for a long time.

"So," Jen said finally. "You still love Josh, huh?"

I didn't bother to deny it; she knew me too well. "Am I that obvious?" I asked.

She shrugged. "I can just tell."

"Well don't worry. I have every intention of getting it under control. I've come way too far to fall back into *that*. I'll get over it."

Jen didn't respond. I wondered if she doubted me.

"Ginny," she said finally, her voice thoughtful. "You *have* come too far to fall back into that." Before I could decide if I was happy she was agreeing or sad that she didn't think Josh and I were made for each other, she continued. "But I don't think you will. You're a totally different person than you were last summer. You have this whole life now, and you're happy in it. You know what makes you happy, what truly satisfies you."

I nodded in the darkness. She was right.

"Sweetie, when you first found out you were pregnant—before Josh had moved and changed his number—why didn't you tell him about the baby?"

I had been afraid of this. Jen had always sensed there was more to the story than I was telling her, and I figured one day she would come right out and ask me. That was just her style.

So I told her everything. I told her how I had been in that last year with Josh, how crazy and out of control I had gotten when I feared he was slipping away. I told her about the partying and the drinking, about how I had no idea who I was when Josh was gone. I told her that, without him, I felt like I needed to fill every quiet moment with some kind of noise, some kind of distraction.

And, because she never interrupted, never said a word—because she just let me talk—I told her about the last party, the guy I had gotten drunk with, and what I had done. When I had finished talking, she reached out and took my hand, squeezing it gently.

"That's not you anymore, Ginny," she said, her voice clear and confident. "It just isn't. Whether you love Josh or not, whether he loves you or not, that is not who you are now. No matter what. Whether you're single or you end up in a relationship, it doesn't really matter. You're not going to go back to that. I know you won't. You don't have to be afraid."

* * *

Josh had left two days later. It was an awkward parting. He didn't want to leave Danny and he had confessed to me that Seattle was not all he hoped it would be. Despite what his mother had bragged to me, the job was little more than an internship, and he hated the weather. He hadn't made many friends, and he was lonely there.

When I walked him to the door that night, there was so much I wanted to say, but I held my tongue. I sensed that he too wanted to talk. We hadn't discussed when he would be back or when he would see Danny again. Everything felt muddled and uncertain. So we hugged awkwardly, he promised to call to check on Danny every night, and he was gone.

Now, nearly a month later, I still felt that uncertainty. Josh called every night like clockwork. At first, the conversation was stilted—I would tell him about Danny and what he had done that day. But, as Danny was only six weeks old, there wasn't a whole lot to tell. So we would politely question each other about our days, and hang up. It was majorly awkward.

As time went on, his calls started to feel more natural. We started talking, like we used to, about everything. He had seen a movie he thought I would like, I had read a book I loved but I knew he would hate. We talked about our jobs. He wanted to know everything about the book store and I was happy to tell him. I told him how much I loved it, how amazing it felt to have responsibilities, to have ideas and to get to put them in motion. I could hear that he was impressed, proud of me even, in his voice. I enjoyed his reaction, but I didn't feel like my life hinged on it.

He still was not talking to his parents. His mother called and left him a message almost every day, crying and begging him to forgive her. She told him she had panicked when she heard my news, and had only ever wanted what was best for him. Incidentally, she had taken the picture of Amy off of Josh's computer. It had been taken at a party for Josh's promotion to editor—a party I myself had attended. Oddly, Josh was nearly as angry about this invasion of privacy as he was about the rest of it.

I couldn't counsel him on what to do where his mother was concerned, as I was prone to fantasies of bashing her head in myself. For now, he was refusing to call her back and I had tentatively invited him to come to us for Thanksgiving.

When I finally got home that night, I found Annie all ready to give Danny his bath. I decided, for once, to let her, choosing instead to make myself some dinner—of course I ate my dinner standing up at the counter watching while he splashed his chubby hands in the bathwater.

When he was dry and in his jammies, I propped him up in his boppy pillow—it turned out LeeAnn at Baby and Me! had been right; the boppy pillow was totally a necessity—and spent the next hour or so playing with him. He loved patty-cake, tummy tickles, the itsy-bitsy-spider—just about any game that required me to touch him would make him laugh.

I felt pretty content. Sure, there were a lot of uncertainties with Josh, but sitting here now, with my baby in my arms, I felt like I was pretty lucky. I figured asking for much more would be tempting fate.

Chapter Forty

Three Months: *Your baby has grown and changed so much since the day he was born. At twelve weeks, your baby is more than likely sleeping better, eating less frequently, laughing and smiling at you, and recognizing your face and voice. Some mommies consider this the 'honeymoon' period with their baby! Enjoy these precious times with him: he'll be grown up before you know it. While you have the chance, spend as much time as you can playing with him—and loving him! He is, after all, your most precious gift!*—Dr. Rebecca Carr, *A Fabulous First Year with Baby!*

"Shut up." Jen walked into the living room, where Annie and I were getting the baby ready, and stopped in her tracks. "Seriously, shut up. Danny, how are you that cute?"

I laughed—she had a point.

It was Halloween, and Annie and I had decided Danny needed to wear a costume to get into the spirit of things. We had taken a green pillowcase and added armholes to the sides. Annie, who had gotten pretty good at sewing when making Danny's crib bedding, had then sewn a hem in the top, leaving only a hole for his neck. We plopped Danny into it, like it was a little sleeping bag. Annie had made three little pillows out of a darker green towel and attached them to his front, and we found a green baby cap that just barely fit him...

"He looks like a pea pod!" Jen exclaimed. "That's adorable!"

"Right?" Annie held him up, laughing. He did look pretty damn adorable, if I do say so myself. And he was in such a good mood tonight, giggling at everything and flashing his toothless grin. I could not get enough of him.

"Ginny, you should come with me," Jen said, flopping down on the couch. She was supposed to be heading to a Halloween party at the office building of her firm that night, but she had done little but complain about it all week.

"And what would I do with the baby?" I asked.

"He could come too! I talk about him so much. Everyone would love to see him."

"No thanks," I said, picking him up and bouncing him on my knees. "Danny and I are gonna chill out here and hand out candy. Plus, I promised some of the neighbors I would bring him by trick-or-treating."

"Fine," she sighed. "Leave me to go and schmooze all by myself, thanks."

"You're welcome," I said cheerily.

"And what about you?" she demanded of Annie. "Where are you off to tonight?"

"I have the Zombie Musical, remember?" Annie asked, standing up and stretching. "I promised I would be an usher." She looked over at the clock. "In fact, I better head down there soon. Let me just get some pictures of the little pea pod first..." She wandered off to find her camera.

"Are you sure you want to stay in alone tonight?" Jen asked me seriously.

"I'm not alone; I've got the little man over here," I told her. "We're going to have a fun night."

"If you're sure." She didn't sound convinced, but she kissed Danny on the cheek and stood. "I guess I better go get ready."

Annie left shortly after, so I brought Danny into Jen's room to keep her company while she got ready. Her costume was some kind of she-devil getup. When it came to fashion, be it Halloween or not, Jen was all about elegance. I knew I would find nothing polyester or nylon in her room. In fact, she was wearing a rather tight, sleeveless red dress that nicely showed off her cleavage—it might have read slutty if not for its knee-length hem. Instead, she looked elegant and sexy. She topped it off with a red horned headband, her only real nod to the holiday. She was a knock-out.

"Any good prospects at this party?" I asked her, lounging with Danny on the bed while she put on her make-up.

Jen snorted. "Yeah right. Everyone at my firm is either female and bitchy or male and gay."

"I thought you said it wouldn't be just work people?"

She shrugged. "Who knows. But from my experience I'm gonna guess it will be disappointing pickings." She pressed her lips together and moved back from the mirror. "How do I look?"

I stood up, bringing Danny with me, to kiss her cheek. "You're hot."

She smiled. "Okay, Danny, give Auntie Jen a kiss." She pecked his cheek, smearing her lipstick a little. "Have fun, sweetie. Call me if you need anything."

"Kay," I replied, walking her to the door. "Have a great night. Be open-minded!"

She rolled her eyes at me as she stepped outside. Danny and I stood in the doorway, watching her until she got into the car. "Just you and me, little man," I told him. I shut the screen but left the front door open, so we could hear the trick-or-treaters.

It was a fun night. Danny was enthralled by the colorful costumes we saw on the kids who came to our door. I brought him around to a few of the neighbors we were close with. Everyone oohed and ahhed over his cuteness, and he ate up the attention.

I was out of candy by eight thirty, so I shut off the porch light and locked the door. I gave Danny his bath and fed him. The excitement of the day had clearly worn him out: he was asleep before I could make it up the stairs.

I decided to make myself some popcorn and see if there were any scary movies on TV. As I pulled the bag from the microwave, I heard the doorbell ring. "Stupid kids," I muttered. I headed to the living room and pulled open the door, prepared to tell whoever it was to clear off.

But it wasn't a kid trick-or-treating.

"Hey, Ginny," said Josh. "Can I come in?"

* * *

Josh had moved home. I couldn't believe it. I had talked to him the night before, and he said nothing about it. But here he was, back in Michigan. He had quit his job in Seattle, bought a plane ticket, and driven straight here from the airport.

"Why didn't you tell me?" I asked, once I had recovered from my shock enough to let him into the house.

He shrugged, walking over to sit on the couch. I joined him. "I wasn't sure what you would think about it."

"Do your parents know?"

He shook his head.

"Well, you just missed Danny; he's fast asleep. He had a pretty big night. Oh, I should find Annie's camera, she took pictures of his costume, you need to see it—" I started to stand but he grabbed my arm and pulled me back down.

"Ginny, hang on. The pictures can wait."

For some reason my heart started to pound and I found it difficult to meet his eyes.

"I want to talk to you," he said quietly. "Will you look at me, please?"

I met his gaze and the intensity of it stirred something deep in my belly.

"What do you want to talk about?" I asked, my voice shaking.

"I love you, Ginny."

It felt like an explosion went off inside my chest. Was I hearing him right? Was this really happening right now?

"Say something, please," he said, reaching over and grabbing my hand.

"I...Josh...I don't know..." I trailed off. There was so much I wanted to say, so many questions I had, but I felt like my brain wasn't connecting to my mouth.

"Ginny, I know you have no reason to want me anymore. I know I treated you horribly and put you through so much. But I love you. I never stopped. I thought about you every day in Seattle, missed you every day."

"Is that why you came back?" I whispered. "Last month, is that what you wanted to tell me?"

He nodded. "But I still didn't know if I was good for you. I was so afraid we'd go back to how we were. I waited as long as I could, hoping I was giving you the chance to move on, but I couldn't take it anymore. I missed you too much. I figured I would come back and see you, and then maybe I would know what to do." He laughed. "And instead I found everything I ever wanted."

His mother had said that to me—that Josh was finally getting everything he had ever wanted. I knew she was wrong then, I had been sure of it.

"I found Danny, and he's perfect, Gin." Josh smiled. "And then there was you. You were so happy, so confident. It was like I was finding the old Ginny, but even better, because you weren't pretending anymore. I'm so proud of you, the way you've been so strong for the baby, and starting your new job. You're so...so *real* now, Ginny. And I think I fell even more in love with you."

Happiness was crashing over me in waves. I couldn't believe this was happening. It was everything I had dreamt of for so long—but, just like Josh had said, it was so much better.

"Ginny," Josh said. I looked up at him. "Why are you crying?" he asked uncertainly. "Say something, Ginny. Please."

I shook my head, my throat too tight to speak.

But Josh misunderstood. His face went white and he pulled his hand back from mine.

"Oh," he whispered. "Oh...okay. I understand. Of course."

He moved to stand up and I could only laugh. He looked down at me in surprise.

"Don't be such an idiot," I said, my voice cracking. "I love you!"

"You do?"

"Of course I do!" I wrapped my arms around him, pulling him close to me, breathing in the scent of him, the feel of him. I had missed him so much.

Josh let out a burst of gleeful laughter and pulled back, taking my face between his hands and staring at me. "Really?" he asked. "You can really forgive me?"

"There's nothing to forgive, Josh," I replied. "We both started over. There's nothing to forgive."

He pulled my face towards his and kissed me. I know this is totally cheesy to say, but, oh well, it's true: kissing Josh felt like coming home.

He pulled me up into his lap, resting his head on my shoulder. "Thank God," he murmured. "I was so afraid you were going to tell me to get out."

I laughed, kissing his hair and nestling closer into his arms.

"Is Annie going to kill me when she finds out?"

"She'll probably try," I admitted. He gave a mock-shudder. "Don't worry. I'll talk to her."

"I owe them a lot, don't I?"

"You have no idea, mister." I paused. "They saved me," I told him quietly. "I don't know if Danny and I would be here without them." He pulled me to him even tighter.

"Thank God," he repeated softly, raising his head up to kiss me again.

I melted into his kiss, feeling the heat start to grow from my belly, spreading out into my fingers and toes. Just before I completely lost my head, I heard a sharp cry from above us.

Josh sighed, pulling back. "Guess I'm going to have to get used to that, huh?"

I jumped off his lap and pulled him up from the couch. "It's not so bad," I told him. "You'll see."

"I can't wait to see him," he said, grabbing my hand and heading to the stairs.

"Josh, wait," I said, pulling on his hand to stop him. "I don't want to get married."

He turned to stare at me. "Um, okay," he said uncertainly, looking at me like I was a crazy person.

"Sorry," I laughed. "I didn't mean it like that...I just meant...I really like my life. I like living here with the girls. I want you to be a part of that, but I think we should take things slow."

He smiled at me. "I can handle that."

"Yeah?"

"Yeah. Actually, I was wondering—do you think Annie or Jen might babysit tomorrow?"

"Why?"

"Because I was hoping I could take you out on a date."

I felt a huge smile spread across my face. "That sounds perfect."

I kissed him once more, softly, before I took his hand and led him upstairs, up to where our baby was waiting for us.

ABOUT THE AUTHOR

Rachel Schurig lives in the metro Detroit area with her dog, Lucy. She loves to watch reality TV and she reads as many books as she can get her hands on. In her spare time, Rachel decorates cakes. This is her first novel.

Don't miss the next book from Rachel
Schurig...

Three Girls and a Wedding

Jen Campbell loves weddings. In fact, she loves
them so much that she became an event planner in
the hopes that she would one day get the chance to
help women create the fairy tale day of their
dreams...Unfortunately, the only thing Jen has been
allowed to plan so far are boring restaurant
openings and children's birthday parties.

When Jen's big break finally comes, she realizes that
wedding planning is a heck of a lot more
complicated than picking out the perfect flowers and
cake.

Add to the chaos a pair of fighting friends, a totally
pressuring mother, and a ridiculously gorgeous (but
moody) best man, and Jen has her work cut out for
her.

In Three Girls and a Wedding, Jen Campbell will try
to plan the perfect wedding and maybe—just
maybe—create her very own happily-ever-after.

Coming Soon

Printed in Great Britain
by Amazon.co.uk, Ltd.,
Marston Gate.